The author has been intrigued by the phenomenon of Latin women's involvement in the East, in matters of politics and governance, during the first sixty years of the Crusaders' presence in the Islamic East. The Crusader women did not actively seek involvement in politics or compete with men for rule. Instead, they found themselves inadvertently entangled in a complex web. The persistence of the Kings of Jerusalem in asserting their authority over all Crusader entities in the Islamic East provided the gateway for Crusader women to assume political leadership through means such as political marriages. In this novel, the author adopted an approach that combines elements of a novel and a play. The author narrated the events through the voices of the Crusader characters themselves. He tried his best to be objective, especially since the novel is relevant to the Crusaders, the opponents of Muslims.

To my beloved kids, Omar and Ghaneemah.

Dr. Jamal M.h. AlZanki

THE RULING OF WOMEN IN THE KINGDOM OF THE LORD

AUSTIN MACAULEY PUBLISHERS
LONDON · CAMBRIDGE · NEW YORK · SHARJAH

Copyright © Dr. Jamal M.h. AlZanki 2024

The right of Dr. Jamal M.h. AlZanki to be identified as author of this work has been asserted by the author in accordance with Federal Law No. (7) of UAE, Year 2002, Concerning Copyrights and Neighboring Rights.

All rights reserved. No part of this publication may be reproduced, stored in a retrieval system, or transmitted in any form or by any means, electronic, mechanical, photocopying, recording, or otherwise, without the prior permission of the publishers.

Any person who commits any unauthorized act in relation to this publication may be liable to legal prosecution and civil claims for damages.

This is a work of fiction. Names, characters, businesses, places, events, locales, and incidents are either the products of the author's imagination or used in a fictitious manner. Any resemblance to actual persons, living or dead, or actual events is purely coincidental.

ISBN – 9789948747284 – (Paperback)
ISBN – 9789948747291 – (E-Book)

Application Number: MC-10-01-9060120
Age Classification: 13+

The age group that matches the content of the books has been classified according to the age classification system issued by the UAE Media Council.

Printer Name: iPrint Global Ltd
Printer Address: Witchford, England

First Published 2024
AUSTIN MACAULEY PUBLISHERS FZE
Sharjah Publishing City
P.O Box [519201]
Sharjah, UAE
www.austinmacauley.ae
+971 655 95 202

Preface

As a researcher specializing in the history of Islamic-Western relations during the Crusades, particularly in their early stages, I was intrigued by the phenomenon of Western women's involvement in the East, especially in matters of politics and governance, during the first sixty years of the Crusader presence in the Islamic East. Therefore, I decided to explore this fascinating and relatively unfamiliar subject. I dedicated two years of my life to studying this captivating topic in medieval history, which, to my knowledge, no researcher—whether Muslim or Christian—has ever delved into.

I became aware that Crusader women did not actively seek involvement in politics or compete with men for rule. Instead, they found themselves inadvertently entangled in this complex web. The persistence of the Kings of the Kingdom of Jerusalem in asserting their authority over all Crusader entities in the Islamic East provided the gateway for Crusader women to assume political leadership through means such as political marriages. Consequently, I found it crucial to discuss this topic while examining the different power struggles, whether among Crusaders or others.

As a result, the title of my study naturally became "The Aspiration of Crusader Women for Power and the Various Power Struggles in the Early Stages of the Crusades."

With the grace of God, I completed my research close to two years ago, and it was approved for publication in the Journal of Literature and Social Science issued by the Council of Scientific Publications, affiliated with the University of Kuwait. It was published in December 2008 under Volume 29, Thesis Number 206.

A few months before publishing the research, I decided to transform it into a narrative that could add excitement and make it more accessible to esteemed Arab readers, helping them grasp this groundbreaking topic. Trusting in God, I embarked on this journey, and through His will, I found inspiration for my mind and pen. Thus, this novel was born in its current form, titled "The Ruling of Women in the Kingdom of the Lord."

In this work, I adopted an approach that combines elements of a novel and a play. This approach helps condense a lengthy period filled with significant and intertwined events and layers, presenting it in an objective, unbiased manner. To achieve this, I chose to narrate it through the voices of the Crusader characters themselves.

I presented this work to a selection of critics and literature enthusiasts, and they embraced the idea.

I hope this novel captures the interest of esteemed Arab readers and, by the grace of Almighty God, will be translated into foreign languages, particularly to familiarize Western readers with this unique phenomenon—a subject overlooked by Western researchers, despite its strong connection to their history, perhaps even more so than to our Islamic history.

May God grant us success.

Kuwait, 8th Shawwal, 1430 AH / 27th September 2008 AD

Dr. Jamāl Muhammad Hasan ʿAbd al-Raḥīm al-Zanki

It is November of the year 1095 AD, and Lord Baldwin of Boulogne is on his way, accompanied by his cousin, Lord Baldwin of Bourg, to attend the Council of Clermont in southern France, at the invitation of Pope Urban II.

They discuss several topics on their way.

Baldwin of Bourg asks his cousin Baldwin of Boulogne about the reasons for their invitation by the Pope to attend a synod, being secular men.

Lord Baldwin of Boulogne responds: "It is speculated that the papacy seeks to garner support from secular feudal lords against their arch-enemy, Henry IV, the ruler of the Holy Roman Empire. Henry has refused to submit to the authority of the papacy and to pledge allegiance, in the feudal manner, to the Pope, as secular followers do to their feudal lords."

Lord Baldwin of Bourg: "But what role can we, the secular barons, play in the Pope's interests against the wishes of our sovereigns, the kings of Latin Europe, to whom we owe loyalty? Does the Pope view us merely as instruments to be used against the kings he opposes?"

Lord Baldwin of Boulogne: "I honestly do not know the true purpose behind this invitation. However, I am certain that there must be a significant matter at hand. Perhaps the secrecy surrounding it was deliberate, and the Pope intends to unveil a surprise during the Council."

Lord Baldwin of Bourg: "Indeed, I find myself perplexed by Pope Urban II's methods. His insistence on making the kings of Latin Europe his secular followers, requiring their allegiance as if they were vassals, has led to the loss of many as his allies. He even issued decisions against Emperor Henry IV, banishing him from the mercy of God, and similarly, our own Lord Philip I, King of France, faced excommunication due to his marriage to Bertrade. The Pope claims it is not permissible for King Philip to marry her without the Pope's approval of her divorce. What a powerful man he is; even our kings are subject to his influence over people's lives. They cannot even seek divorce without his consent."

Lord Baldwin of Boulogne: "Be cautious with your words, my dear cousin. Do you wish to meet the same fate as those rulers, provoking the wrath of God and the threat of hellfire? It appears you have become outspoken. Do you not realize that the Pope has eyes watching us in every corner?"

Lord Baldwin of Bourg: "My apologies, my lord. It was never my intention to show disrespect toward our esteemed Pope. He stands above all earthly judgments, acting in accordance with the divine will, guiding us toward the promised land."

Lord Baldwin of Boulogne: "Enough with this sterile political debate. Let me ask you a personal question, why are you still not married even though you are twenty-five?"

Lord Baldwin of Bourg: "And what would lead me to commit to an act that could leave me bound to a woman giving me orders to follow obediently, akin to a slave to his master, as you are?"

Lord Baldwin of Boulogne: "Well said, cousin. I wish I were single like you, being with any woman I desire, without having to be questioned or controlled by a single woman."

Lord Baldwin of Bourg: "You are still better off than so many others, at least your woman pays no heed to your affairs, as if she does not have a hint of jealousy in her."

Lord Baldwin of Boulogne: "Indeed, that is one of her best qualities, one that I hope she continues to possess."

Right before the Pope takes his place upon the platform in the spacious meadow of Avignon, where flowers bloom beautifully in late autumn near the city of Clermont in southern France, a dialogue unfolds between the two kinsmen: Baldwin of Boulogne and Baldwin of Bourg.

The large crowd gathers, including hundreds of bishops and lords, and dozens of esteemed and famous barons, the most renowned of whom is Count Raymond IV of Toulouse.

Lord Baldwin of Bourg: "We have grown tired of the endless clashes and arguments among the clergy. They cannot even reach a resolution to the simplest of disagreements without the intervention of the Pope, as if they have no power or authority."

Lord Baldwin of Boulogne: "Anyway, we are not here to discuss these trivial matters. We were invited to witness a significant announcement that the Pope will reveal in this promised sermon."

Worn out and weary, Pope Urban II took the stand, wrapped in his cloak. Despite his apparent exhaustion, he continues with fervor and zeal, speaking about the suffering of Christians in the East due to the injustice practiced by Muslims ever since the Seljuks claimed power over the Abbasid Caliphate about fifty years ago.

Pope Urban II: "O sons of Christ, beloved of the Lord, whom His mightiness chose for the salvation of all human souls from original sin... Your sisters in the East are violated and raped... Your brothers, the pilgrims, have their belongings confiscated and are humiliated during their visits to the holy tomb in the Holy City by the enemies of the Lord, the Muslims."

Lord Baldwin of Bourg, addressing Lord Baldwin of Boulogne: "It appears that the Pope has forgotten that these very crimes do occur here in Latin Europe as well, among those who share the same faith (Catholic). Has he overlooked the tragedies caused by the hand of feudal knights who destroy, plunder, steal, and shed the blood of the innocent? They spare no one and nothing from their wickedness, not even our churches. They strip them of their sanctity and turn them into scenes of vice."

Lord Baldwin of Boulogne: "Shut up, you fool! Have you forgotten that we are in the presence of our lord, the Pope?"

Lord Baldwin of Bourg: "I am well-aware of that, but I cannot hold back these emotions gripping my soul just like those who fear speaking the truth to the face of Saint Peter (our Lord Jesus' disciple)."

Pope Urban II, addressing the crowds:

"Here I stand, calling upon you, O chosen ones of the Lord, to set aside your disputes and stand united in heart and mind. Support your Christian brethren in the East who are suffering and liberate the tomb of your Lord in the Holy City from the defilement of renegades. O children of the Lord, take up your weapons and embark on a holy pilgrimage, supplicating to your Lord. Fight your enemies and achieve victory in this life and the Hereafter. The Promised Land of

Milk and Honey awaits you, while you fight in a land that has become constricted, with no room for expansion and the acquisition of new domains."

Lord Baldwin of Bourg, addressing lord Baldwin of Boulogne:

"Indeed, by God, in our eagerness to triumph in this world, we have forgotten about the Hereafter."

Lord Baldwin of Boulogne: "I beseech you, Baldwin, to prepare yourself, for we are about to embark on the holy pilgrimage summoned by the Pope. Join me and my brother, Duke Godfrey, who will undoubtedly partake in this divine endeavor. I perceive it as an enchanting adventure and a splendid opportunity to achieve victory in this world as well as secure our place in the Hereafter, as promised by the Pope."

Returning to the city of Boulogne in northeastern France, Lord Baldwin of Boulogne enters his house, overwhelmed by excitement and fervor after attending the assembly in Clermont. He shares with his wife, Godehilde, the details of the assembly's events, brimming with enthusiasm and determination to participate in this armed pilgrimage.

Lord Baldwin of Boulogne, addressing his wife: "I see that you are as captivated by the divine plan proclaimed by the Pope in that distinguished assembly."

Godehilde: "And who would not be? It concerns a momentous event and a sacred expedition driven by noble principles, decreed by our Pope."

Lord Baldwin of Boulogne: "Indeed, my love, I have taken it upon myself to sacrifice my humble life gladly for our Lord, Jesus Christ, and in unwavering obedience to Pope Urban II."

Godehilde: "I too have pledged myself and all I have as a tribute to our Lord and in steadfast compliance with Pope Urban II."

Lord Baldwin of Boulogne, interrupting: "Yes, my lady, your fervent emotions for this Crusade reflect a sincere love for our Lord. However, you are but a frail woman, and the war in the East might put your life in danger."

Godehilde, resolutely: "I would gladly offer my life and all that I have as a ransom for Christianity and our Lord. I will not allow you to venture alone, vulnerable to the devil's temptations."

Baldwin of Boulogne: "Fear not, my lady, I am a man who fears God. I shall not tarnish my honor or yours during this sacred pilgrimage, a pilgrimage to atone for my sins, as the Pope promised."

Godehilde: "I know, my lord, that you are a God-fearing man. Yet, I also know that even the most degraded women will suddenly repent and join this holy pilgrimage. What a pilgrimage it will be, where the fallen women emerge repentant and sincere, as if they are the most righteous among people."

Lord Baldwin of Boulogne: "I beg of you to carefully consider this matter. The war in the East against the formidable Turks is no stroll or short war; it is going to be a fierce one, possibly lasting for months, if not years."

Godehilde replies with determination: "My mind is set on this. You will not be leaving on your own. I will join you on this holy pilgrimage, no matter what you say. I am prepared to dedicate the remainder of my life to this armed expedition."

Defeated and resigned, Lord Baldwin of Boulogne shakes his head and says: "The Pope has warned us against dissuading anyone from joining the holy pilgrimage, and thus, I will respect your choice."

Lord Baldwin of Boulogne visits his cousin, Lord Baldwin of Bourg, at his residence and complains to him about his wife's insistence on joining the Crusade.

Lord Baldwin of Boulogne: "It appears your envy of my relationship with my wife, who does not harbor a trace of jealousy towards me, has worked against me. There she is, insisting on accompanying me on the Crusade, doubting my devotion to her and stripping away my freedom to act as I wish on this holy pilgrimage, where the noblest men and women are enlisting."

Lord Baldwin of Bourg smirks with a mocking smile: "Thank God I am not married."

Lord Baldwin of Boulogne, continuing: "I will ensure she regrets the day she insisted on joining the Crusade. You will see what I intend to do to her during this pilgrimage she claims to join for the cause, when in reality, her sole purpose is to make my life a living hell and deprive me of innocent affairs with the fairest and most honorable women in Latin Europe!"

On December 23, 1097, the forces of Duke Godfrey, the Duke of Lower Lorraine in northwestern Germany, arrived at the Byzantine capital, Constantinople. He led a contingent of twenty thousand warriors, including ten thousand on horseback, who were strong and brave. Among the prominent leaders were his brother Lord Eustace, Lord Baldwin of Boulogne, his cousin Lord Baldwin of Bourg, and others.

Emperor Alexios Komnenos of the Byzantine Empire insisted on personally meeting with all leaders and obtaining their oath of loyalty. He compelled them to promise to return to him everything they would seize from the Muslims, particularly the territories previously under Byzantine rule.

Oddly enough, prior to Duke Godfrey's arrival, the Norman Prince Bohemond of Taranto in southern Italy, son of Robert Guiscard, had arrived at Constantinople with his army.

It is noteworthy that Bohemond had fought alongside his father in the Byzantine Empire's army led by Emperor Alexios Komnenos in the Balkan lands more than eleven years prior, between 1081 and 1085. They suffered a great defeat, and Bohemond fled back to Taranto after losing his father in the Balkans in 1085. Bohemond was eager to win the favor of Emperor Alexios Komnenos, who was once his enemy. He swiftly took the oath of loyalty without hesitation, but he secretly harbored ulterior motives.

When Duke Godfrey arrived, Bohemond tried to lure him into forming an alliance against the Emperor and taking over the city of Constantinople.

Duke Godfrey was a faithful Christian knight, and he reminded Bohemond that he was part of a divine project called for by the Pope of the Catholic Church. He emphasized that he had not come to fight against his Byzantine brethren.

However, soon Duke Godfrey's forces clashed with the Emperor's troops, and Godfrey had to swear allegiance to the Emperor.

A dialogue unfolds between Lord Baldwin of Boulogne and his brother, Duke Godfrey, where Lord Baldwin criticizes Duke Godfrey's decision to pledge allegiance to the Byzantine Emperor.

Lord Baldwin of Boulogne: "It is astonishing, my lord, how you could agree to pledge allegiance to the Byzantine ruler as if we were merely his mercenaries, serving this villain and aiming to reclaim what the Muslims have seized from his lands."

Duke Godfrey reassures his anxious brother: "Fear not, my brother. Our pledge to this so-called Emperor does not imply submission to him. Our loyalty belongs solely to our Lord, King Philip I of France. As for this Alexios Komnenos, he will not gain our allegiance."

Lord Baldwin of Boulogne expresses relief: "Indeed, I am now reassured about the path of our holy campaign. We embarked to achieve the goals of the Catholic Church and our own objectives, not the aims of those renegade Byzantines."

Duke Godfrey: "Yes, we are here to accomplish our goals in the East and establish domains in the land of the Muslims, which, as the Pope envisions, overflows with milk and honey. We will challenge the Western kings and perhaps even build kingdoms in the East stronger than those in France, Germany, and England."

Lord Baldwin of Boulogne: "Exactly, that is our aspiration, and the papal authority will not deter us from pursuing our personal ambitions. The papacy seeks to use us as a tool against the kings of Latin Europe. We will exploit this conflict between the papacy and the kings to the fullest, achieving our aims at their expense. Yes, this divine project will fulfill our ambitions."

Duke Godfrey: "If only I could live to see the day when I am crowned the king of the Lord's realm."

Lord Baldwin of Boulogne: "You will always find me by your side, offering all my abilities in your service, my lord."

Duke Godfrey: "Thank you, my dear brother. I genuinely appreciate this sense of brotherhood and sincere loyalty. I hope to repay you one day when my dream becomes a reality."

A few days later, the Crusader armies, numbering around forty thousand cavalry and more than thirty thousand infantry, gathered to impose a fierce siege on the Muslim city of Nicaea. This city was located about sixty kilometers southeast of Constantinople and served as the capital of a Muslim kingdom known as the Sultanate of Rum. The Rum Seljuks, followers of the great Seljuks who once ruled over the territories of the Abbasid Caliphate, held dominion extending from the borders of Transoxiana, Iran, and Iraq in the east to the Levant and Anatolia in the west. Most notably, the Rum Seljuks controlled vast portions of Anatolia, with their kingdom sharing a border with a rival Muslim emirate in the northeast, known as the emirate of the Danishmends.

Overall, the Crusaders were under the leadership of several prominent figures. Duke Godfrey and his brother Lord Baldwin of Boulogne led the northern Franks, totaling about twenty thousand. Additionally, Prince Bohemond the Norman, son of Robert Guiscard, and his nephew Tancred, brought five thousand Norman cavalry from southern Italy. Robert, Count of Normandy, from northwest France commanded ten thousand cavalry. Among the leaders,

Raymond IV, Count of Toulouse, represented the southern Franks (Provençals). At fifty years old, he was the eldest of the leaders and had been the first to declare his readiness to participate in the Crusade at the Council of Clermont. His army consisted of eight thousand fighters.

A dialogue unfolds between Duke Godfrey, his brother Lord Baldwin of Boulogne, and their cousin Lord Baldwin of Bourg.

Lord Baldwin of Bourg: "We have endured five weeks of fierce fighting, and these scoundrels are yet to surrender, despite the crushing defeat suffered by their leader, Qilij Arslan, in his recent attempt to break our tight siege of this grand city."

Lord Baldwin of Boulogne: "I have longed for the day when we storm the Holy City of Nicaea, satisfying my desire to witness the blood of the Muslims splatter against the sky and their wicked souls perish."

Duke Godfrey, smiling: "It seems that the storming of this Holy City is merely a matter of days away. This is the same city where the early fathers convened during the time of the Roman Emperor Constantine the Great in the year 325, at the first Ecumenical Council. We shall reclaim this city for the Catholic Church and the Kingdom of God."

Lord Baldwin of Bourg: "I wish I could storm the city now and seize it with my forces, claiming the spoils for myself, away from the rest of the leaders."

Lord Baldwin of Boulogne: "You mean to share the spoils with us, your relatives, undoubtedly?"

Lord Baldwin of Bourg, correcting: "I apologize, my lord, I did not mean that I would claim them solely for myself and exclude you."

The next morning, to everyone's surprise, the Byzantine flags were raised over the city of Nicaea. The Muslim defenders had handed over the city to the Byzantine garrison accompanying the Crusade campaign. An arrangement had been made between the Muslims and the Byzantines without the knowledge of the Crusaders. This turn of events infuriated the Crusader leaders, as they were deprived of their first opportunity to exact revenge on the Muslims by killing them and looting their wealth. Furthermore, they were denied the chance to exploit this magnificent city with its abundant resources and breathtaking natural surroundings.

A dialogue takes place between Duke Godfrey, his brother Lord Baldwin of Boulogne, and their cousin Lord Baldwin of Bourg.

Lord Baldwin of Bourg, mockingly: "You see, we have made great sacrifices and spared no effort to seize this magnificent city, only to witness its surrender to the treacherous Byzantines. Is it fair that we put forth everything within our capacity to liberate this city, only for it to be handed over to these Byzantine traitors?"

Duke Godfrey answers: "Let not your heart be troubled by what is lost from the city, for God shall grant us something better. I have heard that Alexios will compensate us for all that we have endured during the siege. We shall not let future opportunities slip by, and our efforts will not be in vain, nor will they solely benefit the Byzantines."

Then the Muslim king, Qilij Arslan, led his cavalry and launched a fierce surprise attack on the disorganized Crusader forces, moving haphazardly in Anatolia. Duke Godfrey's and Count Toulouse's forces, led by Raymond IV, were advancing ahead of the others by more than twenty-four kilometers. They were followed by Bohemond, the Prince of Taranto, leading his troops, along with the forces of Robert, Count of Normandy, and Robert, Count of Flanders, among other leaders. The Muslim forces under King Qilij Arslan almost secured an easy victory over Duke Godfrey's and Count Raymond IV's forces. However, the timely arrival of the Crusader forces under the leadership of Bohemond after three hours turned what could have been a defeat into a significant victory near Dorylaeum on July 1st, 1097. Following this major victory for the Crusaders, no Muslim force dared to attempt stopping the march of the Crusaders until they reached the Muslim city of Antioch, where they laid siege in late October.

After this bitter experience, the Crusader leaders made a decision that no leader could separate from the main army without the approval of the other leaders. The Crusader armies then marched southeast, crossing Anatolia and heading toward the northern lands of the Levant. Despite the advice of the Byzantine guides accompanying them, the Crusader leaders took a shortcut to save time. This led them to a barren desert, the Tarkia desert, where they endured three days of severe thirst. Tragically, five hundred pregnant women perished, and nursing mothers threw their infants to volunteer wet nurses out of sheer desperation. The breasts of these women dried up due to severe thirst, and the volunteer nurses breastfed the babies in a scene witnessed by men. Modesty was disregarded due to the intense hunger the nursing infants were experiencing.

Godehilde, the wife of Lord Baldwin of Boulogne, engages in conversation with him after witnessing this distressing scene.

Godehilde: "Never in my life had I imagined I would witness such a petrifying scene, where women have to resort to breastfeeding infants in such a distressing manner."

Lord Baldwin of Boulogne: "I have repeatedly told you, my lady, that this is a serious campaign with great challenges. I advised against your participation, but you were insistent."

Godehilde: "My decision to take part in this campaign and face its difficulties is not something I regret. However, seeing the suffering of these women and their infants saddens me deeply. Yet, my faith in the divine project and the liberation of our Lord's tomb remains steadfast and even stronger."

Lord Baldwin of Boulogne: "Your unwavering faith in Christ's cause and the necessity of liberating the holy tomb in the Holy Land is indeed growing stronger. What a sincere woman you are!"

Godehilde: "Yes, my faith remains unshaken, and I am more determined than ever to accompany you. I want to ensure that your attention does not stray towards those women who shamelessly parade around, moving from one tent to another, offering themselves and their honor as a sacrifice for the Crusader cause. How cheap are their principles and their religion, and how cowardly are the clergy who do not move a muscle to prevent them from spreading vice in the divine project."

Lord Baldwin of Boulogne: "I have been nothing but a faithful husband and a loyal Christian, and you still think badly of me!"

Not even two weeks had passed since the Crusader leaders pledged, following the Battle of Dorylaeum, not to separate any force from the main army, when both Baldwin of Boulogne and Baldwin of Bourg separated with their forces, which amounted to seven hundred knights, from the main army. The forces of Tancred, representing the Norman forces coming from southern Italy and led by Bohemond the Norman, separated first and were fewer in number than the forces of Baldwin of Boulogne. After their separation, they headed towards the fortress of Tarsus in the province of Cilicia in southeastern Anatolia. The inhabitants of the city, Armenians, surrendered the fortress to Tancred after the Muslim garrison fled. The forces of Baldwin of Boulogne arrived at Tarsus shortly after, where Tancred gave them a warm welcome.

Then a dialogue takes place between Lord Baldwin of Boulogne and his cousin Lord Baldwin of Bourg in the fortress of Tarsus.

Lord Baldwin of Bourg: "I can see the Normans of Italy intending to plunder the spoils from us Franks. Look at Tancred; he has taken Tarsus without any difficulty. Perhaps he will even occupy all the fortresses in the province of Cilicia and establish the first Norman Crusader principality in the Muslim lands of southeastern Anatolia."

Lord Baldwin of Boulogne: "Indeed, my dear, a surge of rage gripped me when I saw the Normans' flags fluttering over that fortress. How I wished to tear them down and hoist our own flags in their place."

Lord Baldwin of Bourg: "Just give the word, my lord, and I will rip those devilish flags down. We can expel Tancred and his arrogant warriors who have dared to raise their banners without a thought for our esteemed Duke Godfrey and his Frankish forces."

Lord Baldwin of Boulogne: "I fear that such action could create division among our leaders. We are on a holy pilgrimage that has not yet fulfilled its primary goals, particularly the liberation of the holy tomb."

Lord Baldwin of Bourg: "I will stand by your side, my lord, and present you as the wronged, not the wrongdoer. We can justify it by claiming we are acting under the command of Duke Godfrey, asserting that we promised to hand over every liberated city from the Muslims to him."

Lord Baldwin of Boulogne: "Thank you, my dear, for suggesting this bold and clever idea, even though it may carry significant consequences."

Lord Baldwin of Bourg led a contingent of his forces, swiftly pulling down the pennons of the southern Normans and hoisting up the oriflammes of the Franks. Tancred, incensed by this discourteous act, left Tarsus with his troops and headed towards the stronghold of Mamistra. Meanwhile, a Norman force of three hundred knights arrived from Antioch, sent by his uncle Bohemond, to Tarsus, which Tancred had just vacated. Baldwin of Boulogne denied them entry and left them outside the castle walls. That night, the Norman forces remained unprotected outside the fortress, and Lord Baldwin of Boulogne did not even provide them with food. However, the castle's residents, who were Armenians, took pity on these knights and lowered food to them using ropes, all without Lord Baldwin of Boulogne's knowledge.

As fate would have it, the last Muslim Turkish garrison slipped out of the castle under the cover of night, taking the women and children with them, without alerting Lord Baldwin of Boulogne's forces. After securing their families, they returned and attacked the Norman host that had come from Bohemond while they were asleep, catching them off guard.

When the soldiers awoke in the morning and saw this horrifying scene, they were furious. The lives of these knights were lost due to Baldwin of Boulogne's arbitrary actions. The soldiers rose up, drawing their swords against him, and advanced towards him in anger over the brutal killing of their Norman brethren.

Lord Baldwin of Bourg stands among the soldiers, addressing them in defense of his cousin Lord Baldwin of Boulogne.

Lord Baldwin of Bourg: "Hold on, O great lords… You, who have forsaken the pleasures of this world for a holy pilgrimage, following in the footsteps of our Lord Christ—how can you rush to judge our revered Lord Baldwin of Boulogne? Accusing him of ignoring the divine project and neglecting to preserve the lives of your knightly brethren who came to serve the Lord last night? Our leader, Baldwin of Boulogne, did not deny them entrance unless it was in fulfillment of the solemn oath he took to Lord Duke Godfrey. He vowed not to permit anyone to enter lands he conquers in Godfrey's name without explicit permission."

One of the angered soldiers stands up and says:

"No... He acted only for his own interests, without seeking Lord Duke Godfrey's permission. The duke carries more mercy and compassion in his heart for his brothers than this man, who seemed indifferent to shedding the blood of these poor knights—victims of his cruelty."

Baldwin of Boulogne stands confidently before his soldiers and says:

"Yes, my lords, everything our great leader Baldwin of Bourg mentioned is true. I adhere to the commands of Lord Duke Godfrey without exception. When I departed my homeland in Bouillon and my estates, it was fueled by love for our Lord and a dedication to the divine cause—a cause championed by our Father, Pope Urban II, at the Council of Clermont two years prior."

The soldiers' anger subsides, and they disperse after Baldwin of Bourg's skillful intervention.

Later, Baldwin of Boulogne and his cousin Baldwin of Bourg find themselves alone, speaking freely.

Lord Baldwin of Boulogne: "Your loyalty as a soldier is unwavering, cousin. Your clever justification for these soldiers, who may lack understanding, has impressed me greatly."

Lord Baldwin of Bourg: "I hope to convince Duke Godfrey that every effort was made to protect Christ's soldiers, as his approval is crucial. As for these naive soldiers, they can be easily swayed."

Lord Baldwin of Boulogne: "Indeed, his approval holds great weight. I also hope that other leaders will rally to our cause, just as you have done. Your honorable stance will be remembered."

Lord Baldwin of Bourg: "Do not dwell on this, my lord. I will work to persuade them. I hope our tensions with the obstinate Tancred do not escalate. He seems resistant to submission, even when those above him in rank and power attempt to assert their authority—much like his uncle Bohemond."

After Tancred departed the fortress of Tarsus with his forces, he made his way to the coast where he encountered new Crusader reinforcements from Flanders and Frisia. Persuading those forces to join him, he bolstered his numbers by several hundred. Empowered by the additional troops, he set his sights on the fortress of Mamistra, which was under the control of the Seljuk Turks. Tancred captured it by force. Following this success, Baldwin of Boulogne once again directed his forces towards Mamistra, aiming to wrest it from Tancred, just as he had previously done with Tarsus.

While marching toward Mamistra, a conversation unfolds between Baldwin of Boulogne and his cousin, Baldwin of Bourg.

Lord Baldwin of Bourg: "It seems, my lord, that this daring move of yours will escalate our troubles with the Normans, especially Bohemond. What he did twelve years ago in the Balkans could not be forgotten. His Norman forces nearly wiped out the large Byzantine army led by Emperor Alexios Komnenos himself."

Lord Baldwin of Boulogne: "Indeed, we maybe more numerous than the Normans of southern Italy in this Holy

Crusade, but our competence may not surpass theirs. Nonetheless, our journey to the East is driven by our own ambitions, even if it means clashing with the fierce Normans."

A fierce battle erupted between the forces of Baldwin of Boulogne and Tancred. In this clash, Baldwin of Boulogne prevailed over Tancred's troops, inflicting heavy casualties and capturing many of his men. Following this confrontation, wise men from both sides intervened, acting as mediators, which eventually led to a reconciliation. The prisoners were released, and Lord Tancred returned angrily to the main Crusader army camped at Marash, reuniting with his uncle Bohemond's forces. Learning about what transpired with his nephew's forces, Prince Bohemond was consumed by fury. Meanwhile, Baldwin of Boulogne led his forces on a visit to his brother, Duke Godfrey, at Marash. He claimed his purpose was to inquire about Godfrey's health, given the injury he sustained during a brawl with a wild bear. In truth, Baldwin's underlying motive was to manipulate his brother Godfrey's sentiments and turn him against their rival, Tancred. However, as he journeyed toward Marash to rendezvous with the main army, he received the somber news of his wife Godehilde's passing.

The two cousins, Baldwin of Boulogne and Baldwin of Bourg, engage in a conversation.

Lord Baldwin of Bourg: "I could not fathom the coldness of your feelings and the dullness of your emotions. It seemed you cared so little when you heard the news of your wife's passing, as if the holy matrimony that bound you two held no significance for you."

Lord Baldwin of Boulogne: "I feigned my grief for her death in a hollow way in front of the soldiers, so that they would see how tender my heart was, but my expressions were faint and betrayed my lack of love for her."

Lord Baldwin of Bourg: "I pray to God for her soul's mercy, as she sincerely participated in this holy endeavor and was dedicated to shielding you from the allure of beautiful and pious women! May He grant you a woman who truly loves you to replace her."

Lord Baldwin of Boulogne: "This love you speak of has not found its place in my heart yet. Women's affections were never my focus. I will marry a woman who brings me the wealth and spoils I need to accomplish my goals and aspirations in this Holy Crusade."

Lord Baldwin of Bourg: "I marvel at you for this tepid religious feeling that you disclose from time to time, but it seems that you, my dear, are not one to care about religion and noble values."

Lord Baldwin of Boulogne: "Spare me the preaching, for we are pursuing our goals in accordance with our righteous religion!"

Lord Baldwin of Bourg: "I hope I live to the day when I see you as a crowned king on the Holy Sepulchre and I crown myself on one of the emirates in the East. I will never forsake you, my dear, for I owe everything to you, and I will never leave your side."

Lord Baldwin of Boulogne: "Your unwavering loyalty and sincere love mean a great deal to me. I long for the day when I attain my wishes, so I can repay you the kindness you have shown me."

On October 13, 1097, Baldwin of Boulogne appeared before his brother, Godfrey, accompanied by a few of his followers. Most of his leaders declined to join him and take his side against Tancred. Baldwin of Boulogne, quite cunning, did not fail to show his grief for the loss of his wife, Godehilde. He also displayed keen concern inquiring about the health of his brother, Godfrey, who had suffered a violent bear attack in the region of Pisidia two months prior. Baldwin of Boulogne attempted to sway his brother to his side in the conflict with Tancred, but his efforts failed miserably.

Lord Baldwin of Boulogne speaks to his brother, Duke Godfrey, in the presence of their cousin Lord Baldwin of Bourg.

Duke Godfrey: "It seems that you have acted foolishly with Tancred. I hope you will refrain from such actions in the future. We Franks have set out faithfully in this holy pilgrimage to achieve our noble goals by noble means, and it is not in our favor to engage in conflicts with our Norman brothers from southern Italy. They share our kingdom in northwestern France and rule over southern Italy. Our good relations with them are essential, as they also have strong ties with the papacy. Straining these relations might cost us the papal support we need in achieving the goals of our 'divine' project."

Baldwin of Boulogne feigned regret in front of his brother Godfrey for his actions against Tancred.

Baldwin of Boulogne: "Yes, my Lord Godfrey, I wholeheartedly agree with what you said. I repent for my behavior and pledge to stay true to the path of righteousness.

Such incidents will not recur in the future. In fact, I intend to join the forces marching towards the city of Antioch in service to God's cause."

Baldwin of Boulogne and his cousin Baldwin of Bourg left Duke Godfrey's assembly showing insincere respect to their master.

A private dialogue takes place between the two cousins.

Lord Baldwin of Bourg: "It seems, my lord, that you are a cunning fox who changes colors and adapts according to the circumstances. Had your allies supported your stance against Tancred, you might have persisted. However, in this instance, you have stepped back temporarily, waiting for the opportune time to resume your confrontation."

Lord Baldwin of Boulogne: "You are correct, my cousin, master of cunning and cleverness. I will not relentlessly seek revenge against the despicable Tancred. My actions are calculated, and my aim is to humiliate him without compromising our larger objectives."

Lord Baldwin of Bourg asks eagerly and curiously: "Will you really join the army of God that will lay siege on the fortified city of Antioch soon? Or will you head to Tarsus, which is under your control, and distract yourself from the objectives of this divine project—to liberate the tomb of our Lord Christ and the Promised Land?"

Lord Baldwin of Boulogne: "Know well, my dear Baldwin, that I always think only of my interest. I seek to achieve my personal interest from this divine campaign. While it carries the sword to relieve the suffering of our Christian brethren in the East, I also see the opportunity to establish the first Latin emirate in a region where the influence of the Muslim Seljuk Sultanate is weak. The inhabitants are

Armenians, our fellow Christians. I seek to make my conquest far from the reach of the leaders of the campaign who vie for authority of the divine campaign and lack unified leadership."

Lord Baldwin of Boulogne departed with his forces for Tarsus, merely two weeks after his visit to his brother Duke Godfrey in Marash. During the visit, he pledged to join the Crusader army marching towards the city of Antioch. However, he remained in Tarsus for over three months, without seeking approval from the Crusade leaders. This once again confirmed his determination to pursue his individual goals, emphasizing his disregard for the collective Crusader project.

Later, towards the end of February in the year 1098, he journeyed to the city of Edessa in Upper Mesopotamia. He was invited by his Armenian ally, a man named Bagrat, who painted a favorable picture of the alliance between Baldwin and the Armenian prince of Edessa, Thoros.

Baldwin of Boulogne paid no attention to the decree by the Crusader leaders that forbade separation from the main army without their authorization. He also dismissed the taunts of his adversary, Tancred, who, along with his uncle Bohemond, would later play a significant role in capturing Antioch. This event occurred after a grueling seven-month-long siege and fierce battles against its defenders.

A dialogue unfolds between Lord Baldwin of Bourg and Lord Baldwin of Boulogne as they journey to the city of Edessa.

Lord Baldwin of Bourg: "My Lord, you are toying with fire; I believe your actions will only stoke your brother's doubts about your loyalty to this divine project."

Lord Baldwin of Boulogne: "Have no fear for my brother, for he possesses a noble heart. Justifying my decision not to join the Lord's army, which is marching to seize the city of Antioch, will demand little effort on my part."

Lord Baldwin of Bourg: "I hold hope that we can persuade our Armenian allies in Edessa to overthrow their leader, Prince Thoros. I have learned that he follows the Orthodox faith, in contrast to his adherents who espouse the Monophysite belief in the singular nature of our Lord Jesus Christ."

Lord Baldwin of Boulogne: "I shall shower our Armenian allies with gold until we rid ourselves of that senile fool, Thoros."

Lord Baldwin of Boulogne approaches the walls of Edessa with his forces and is welcomed by its prince, Thoros. The prince perceives in Baldwin a potential ally against the threat posed by the Seljuk Turks. It appears that Prince Thoros reluctantly agrees to the idea of adopting Baldwin of Boulogne as his son, under pressure from his Armenian court. Given that Thoros lacks an heir, he extends the offer of adoption to Baldwin. Without hesitation, Lord Baldwin of Boulogne promptly accepts this proposition.

As events unfold, it becomes evident that the Armenian conspirator Pakrad had conspired with Prince Thoros's court.

The conspiracy originated with Thoros's decision to adopt Baldwin of Boulogne and involve him in the governance of Edessa. It culminated in a military coup, initiated by these very Armenians, who besieged their master in his residence overlooking one of the city's towers.

In this scene, Thoros hurriedly approaches Lord Baldwin of Boulogne, seeking his aid to break the siege against him. The ensuing dialogue unfolds between them.

Prince Thoros: "Help… Help… My son, do you hear the demands of these ungrateful bastards? I have dedicated my entire life to them, and now they ask that I relinquish my rule."

Lord Baldwin of Boulogne: "Indeed, sir. They are requesting that you step down from your esteemed emirate. Their ingratitude is truly astounding."

Thoros: "Come now, my faithful son. The time has come for you to demonstrate your loyalty to me—the one who adopted you, shared my rule, and promised you my emirate upon my passing. Command your forces to quell these rebels."

Lord Baldwin of Boulogne replies hesitantly: "This is the moment when I must prove my loyalty to you, my lord. However, you know, sir, how much I dread causing harm to my Armenian brethren. I joined this holy war to combat the infidel Muslims, not to fight against my Christian kin, the Armenians."

Prince Thoros, his anger simmering, retorts: "You are proving yourself unworthy of adoption. It is you who incited my followers against me and orchestrated this treacherous coup. These people would never have dared to challenge me, not during the three years I have ruled them. They were loyal until your accursed arrival disrupted our peaceful land, sparking this change. You Crusaders boast of your faithfulness to your Lord Christ and your commitment to covenants—does this mockery reflect your loyalty and faithfulness?"

Lord Baldwin of Boulogne responds with sarcasm: "Indeed, we stand true to our covenants. We arrived solely to liberate you from the Muslims who oppressed you for over four centuries."

Thoros: "Woe to those who so readily betray their allies. I implore the Lord to curse you and exact revenge upon you all, allowing the Muslims to triumph over you. Even they have not displayed the injustice and treachery you have, not even two weeks after I adopted you."

Thoros hurries to grab a rope and lowers himself from the side that the rebels have not yet surrounded. He descends to save himself from those who have revolted against him. At this moment, Lord Baldwin of Boulogne reveals his true colors and rushes to inform the conspiring leaders of Thoros's whereabouts. They swiftly move to execute him, employing the most nefarious method of killing. Then, the rebels rush towards Lord Baldwin of Boulogne, who feigns sorrow for the death of his adoptive father, allowing them to proceed with their plot.

The conspiring leaders then ask Lord Baldwin of Boulogne to accept their rule over the emirate. He shows hesitation but eventually yields to their persistence. Thus, in March of the year 1098, the first Crusader state is established in Armenian lands that belong to the Christian Byzantine Empire, not on Muslim soil. The conspiracy becomes the inaugural means to establish this entity within the framework of the Crusader divine project.

In the evening following Count Baldwin of Boulogne's ascension to the rule of the county of Edessa, a dialogue takes place between him and his cousin, Lord Baldwin of Bourg.

Count Baldwin of Boulogne: "I must confess, cousin, I am impressed by the great skill you have shown in inciting these rascals against their naive lord."

Lord Baldwin of Bourg: "You deserve the credit, my lord, for you are the one who taught me the arts of cunning, or should I say, prudence and diplomacy."

A few days after assuming the rule of the county of Edessa, Baldwin of Boulogne marries an Armenian woman named Arda, the daughter of one of the Armenian leaders also named Thoros. Following the wedding ceremony, a dialogue unfolds between Count Baldwin of Boulogne and his cousin, Lord Baldwin of Bourg.

Lord Baldwin of Bourg: "I find myself perplexed, as you have not chosen a beautiful woman befitting your position and high status among the Latin leaders in the East."

Count Baldwin of Boulogne: "I had hoped for greater discernment and intelligence from you, my dear cousin. Do you believe I have any interest in women? I married this woman, this haggard crone, solely to gain control of her father's money. Thoros the fool appeared on the wedding day as senseless and ignorant—both in his pitiable appearance and his incomprehensible speech."

Lord Baldwin of Bourg: "You tread on thin ice, dear cousin; it seems you have forgotten that I am the genius who cannot be outwitted by even the craftiest of schemers."

Count Baldwin of Boulogne: "I offer my most sincere apologies for this unwarranted disrespect to your esteemed position, a position that has never been nor will be shaken by such misunderstandings."

Lord Baldwin of Bourg: "Please accept my apology as well, sir. I deeply regret the misunderstanding and hope you regard me favorably moving forward. Our bond as cousins and childhood friends remains unshakable, undeterred even by this disagreement."

Count Baldwin of Boulogne: "You will soon witness my dealings with these Armenian scoundrels and how I will teach them a lesson for betraying their late prince, Thoros."

Lord Baldwin of Bourg, interjecting: "Undoubtedly, you are a brilliant man and a seasoned leader with a clear vision and impeccable execution."

Count Baldwin of Boulogne: "Time will show that I am capable of following through on my promises and achieving not only my goals but also yours—the objectives of our mission as Crusaders in these sacred lands, the very lands of our ancestors and forefathers."

A fortnight after this initial meeting, Count Baldwin of Boulogne summoned all Armenian dignitaries and lords in Edessa for an emergency gathering. Crusader leaders, led by Baldwin of Bourg, were also present. Count Baldwin of Boulogne stood as a persuasive orator before this large assembly.

Count Baldwin of Boulogne: "O noble sires, I have come to learn of a plot forming against the one whom you willingly chose to lead you in this holy land. It has become clear that some among you have abandoned the righteous path and conspired with our Muslim foes against us, your Latin brethren."

Thoros the Armenian rises to reply to his kinsman Count Baldwin of Boulogne:

"My lord count, you are well aware that we willingly offered ourselves and our realms to you as our ruler. We collaborated to overthrow our former prince, Thoros. Should not you consider showing gratitude and recognition for our support and cooperation? Or would you prefer that we regret the instant we trusted you to aid us against our Muslim enemies?"

Lord Baldwin of Bourg, interrupting Thoros:

"It is you who orchestrated this plot, and my lord has confirmed that you and those present are conspiring against the rule of your Latin brethren who hold you in high regard."

Thoros retorts sharply: "Baldwin of Bourg, it is you who are influencing our lord count to oppose us. Your intention seems to be to place yourself as the sole commander and advisor to the Count."

Count Baldwin of Boulogne intervenes, interrupting: "Anyhow, this is not the appropriate setting for personal disputes and baseless accusations. I am resolute in my determination to rid my county of traitors who collaborate with our Muslim enemies."

Thoros protests strongly: "You claim a plot against you, but have you presented any evidence to support your accusations?"

Baldwin of Bourg defends his lord, the Count: "All indications point to a plot against my lord, and you seem to be at the forefront of the conspirators."

Thoros responds: "Count, how can you level accusations at the innocent based on unfounded claims? It appears, my lord Count, that you are inclined to dismiss your Armenian brothers from your forces, especially since the troops led by your brother Duke Godfrey joined you after he visited our land a few weeks ago. Proceed then, and cast us aside, your Armenian brothers, trading our friendship and alliance at a meager price. Yesterday, you rid yourself of your adoptive father, poor Prince Thoros; today, you seek to rid yourself of me, your father-in-law, Thoros, and your Armenian brethren."

Count Baldwin of Boulogne feels shame toward his father-in-law and says: "I beg your pardon, my dear father. I did not intend to directly accuse you of plotting. However, rumors suggest that if you were not the instigator, you remained silent about the fall of my rightful county. This county came to your aid and that of your offspring, saving you from the imminent threat posed by the Muslims."

Here, Thoros also tries to express a measure of leniency in his stance, out of concern for himself and his daughter Arda, who is under the guardianship of Baldwin of Boulogne.

Thoros: "I pray, my son, that those who incite discord will not tarnish our friendship. We share a common faith, and I pledge my loyalty to your lordship. As proof, I renounce the rest of my daughter's dowry and offer twenty thousand bezants from my own wealth to your fledgling county, established to fulfill the will of the Lord."

At this point, tensions ease within Count Baldwin of Boulogne, who responds diplomatically.

Count Baldwin of Boulogne: "I hope that misunderstandings will not disturb the tranquility of our goodwill. I thank my generous father for his generosity and his loyalty to us, the sincere Latins who love the Lord."

The clamorous meeting concludes, and the Armenian leaders depart with bowed heads, lamenting the day they placed trust in the Crusaders to liberate them from the tyranny of their former Muslim rulers. On the eve of that eventful day, Count Baldwin of Boulogne encounters his wife, who is filled with anger over what transpired with her father. He expresses profound remorse for the harm inflicted upon her father, shifting the blame to Baldwin of Bourg as the instigator of the discord meant to drive a wedge between him and his loyal father-in-law, who remained faithful to the Latins.

Countess Arda: "It seems you have crossed a line with my father, whose support granted you rule over Edessa, only to repay him with a sinister recompense."

Baldwin of Boulogne: "I offer my heartfelt apology for hurting your dear father. For my father-in-law, Thoros, is the most loyal among my Armenian allies. The greatest blessing he bestowed upon me was you, my beloved countess."

Countess Arda: "It is the first time I have heard such a compliment from you. You have never praised my beauty before."

Baldwin of Boulogne: "Who would dare to question the beauty that captured my heart the moment I laid eyes on you?"

Countess Arda: "It seems you have acquired new skills in flattery and compliments. I am guessing your infamous cousin was your instructor."

Baldwin of Boulogne: "Let us not dwell on that fool. Instead, let me show you the sincerity of my love and the depth of my passion."

Countess Arda: "Well, I hope what I am hearing is truly genuine."

A few days after these tender words, Count Baldwin of Boulogne expropriated a substantial amount of money from his Armenian subjects and coerced them into paying enormous fines. These payments were essentially in return for the privilege of remaining in their own country, as if he were bestowing this grace upon them. Thus, this marked the end of the honeymoon period between the Crusaders and the Armenians in Edessa, and signaled the beginning of a period of woe and sorrow.

Baldwin of Boulogne then utilized the money he confiscated from the Armenian noblemen and leaders of Edessa—an amount valued at twenty thousand gold coins—to expand his fledgling county. He annexed the fortresses of Saruj and Samosata to his domain.

In June of the year 1099, news reached Count Baldwin of Boulogne that the Crusader leaders, including his brother Duke Godfrey, had laid siege to the city of Jerusalem. Despite their struggles due to shortages of horses and soldiers caused by plagues that afflicted them both before and after their capture of the city of Antioch in July 1098, their besieging forces for Jerusalem were estimated at twenty thousand. Meanwhile, their forces that besieged Antioch—less than two years prior in October 1097—surpassed seventy thousand fighters.

This dialogue takes place between Count Baldwin of Boulogne and his cousin Baldwin of Bourg.

Lord Baldwin of Bourg: "Oh, how I long to stand beside my brave brothers in arms as they lay siege to the Holy City, the residence of our Savior Christ, and the ultimate goal of the sacred mission that our Lord the Pope has summoned us for."

Count Baldwin of Boulogne: "And what prevents you from joining your gallant brethren? Do you wish to be like our cowardly adversary Bohemond, who abandoned his Crusader comrades to endure the trials of war? He left to liberate the Holy City only to engage in a dispute with Raymond IV, Count of Toulouse, over the rule of Ma'arrat Nu'man six months ago. He retreated to Antioch to expel the remaining garrison of Raymond, his rival for control of the city, and seized power over the principality of Antioch."

Lord Baldwin of Bourg: "I would never forsake you, my lord and patron. How could I leave you alone to face these conniving Armenians and the Muslim Turks?"

Count Baldwin of Boulogne: "I have curtailed the influence of these Armenians, removing their authority completely to eliminate any chance of a new conspiracy against me in my resolute county. For this, I thank the Lord. You are now free to choose, but I would be honored if you joined the forces of Christ besieging the Holy City on my behalf. I need to avoid being labeled as the man who shunned his duty and deserted the sepulcher of Christ and the purpose of our sacred mission."

Lord Baldwin of Bourg: "It seems, my lord, that you seek to use me as a way to cleanse yourself of the stain of not joining the forces of the Lord that you abandoned two years ago when your unwarranted conflict with our rival Tancred began."

Count Baldwin of Boulogne: "And to me, cousin, it seems you dwell on the past, forgetting your treachery and schemes against the Armenians. Lives were lost, and wealth was taken—a small price, in your eyes, offered as a trivial sacrifice."

Lord Baldwin of Bourg: "I apologize, my lord, for overstepping my bounds in addressing your esteemed position. You are my benefactor and my guide in virtues and sacrifices for the sake of Christ!"

Count Baldwin of Boulogne: "Yes, that is the disciple I expect you to be—compliant and courteous, as you once were. Display the same well-mannered respect you have shown your master."

After six weeks of besieging the city of Jerusalem, the Crusaders managed to capture it by force. They mistreated the defenders of the city and its Muslim inhabitants, committing a horrifying massacre against them. Then, a messenger arrived to Count Baldwin of Boulogne's camp from his brother, Duke Godfrey, bringing him the joyful tidings of Godfrey's conquest of the Holy City and the acceptance of the Crusader leaders for him to be the ruler of the newly acquired kingdom of the Lord.

A dialogue unfolds between the messenger George, Count Baldwin of Boulogne, and his cousin Lord Baldwin of Bourg.

Messenger George: "This is a letter from my lord, the Defender and Guardian of the Holy Sepulchre, Duke Godfrey. Please accept it, my lord."

Count Baldwin of Boulogne receives the letter, reading it carefully. He rejoices at its contents, detailing the efforts the Crusaders invested in occupying the Holy City. The letter recounts the events that unfolded, highlighting Duke Godfrey's significant role in the conflict, particularly in the intense clashes that occurred within Al-Aqsa Mosque, where many of the city's beleaguered residents sought refuge.

As Count Baldwin of Boulogne reads, his cousin Lord Baldwin of Bourg interjects.

Lord Baldwin of Bourg: "I wish I were at the Duke's side to demonstrate my loyalty and dedication to the holy war. I would show him my utmost aversion towards the Muslims."

Messenger George: "My lord, the leaders who engaged in this war spared no effort in displaying their sincerity and deep-seated animosity toward our adversaries. Lord Tancred, in particular, nearly matched Duke Godfrey in his resolute pursuit of the enemy's defeat."

Upon hearing the name Tancred, Count Baldwin of Boulogne's displeasure is evident, but he swiftly attempts to correct his reaction, fearing the messenger might relay this to his brother Duke Godfrey.

Lord Baldwin of Bourg: "I yearn to stand alongside my lord Duke, the Guardian of the Holy Sepulchre. I wish to be his steadfast ally against those who may claim to fight for

God's love but harbor hidden agendas to serve their own interests."

Count Baldwin of Boulogne: "How I long to be near my brother, the Duke, to support him in his honest pursuit alongside our devoted brothers, united in our fight against the foes of Christianity."

Baldwin of Bourg, correcting himself: "Indeed, they are sincere men driven by their love for God and the divine mission. Particularly our brother Tancred, an exemplar of virtue, who alongside his uncle Prince Bohemond, played a pivotal role in liberating both Antioch and the Holy City from our adversaries."

Count Baldwin of Boulogne: "I request that you convey my gratitude to my lord Duke, the Guardian of the Holy Sepulchre, for this letter and the joyous news of our victory. Please assure him of my unwavering commitment to supporting his rule within his sacred realm and aiding in its expansion. Additionally, inform him that I intend to visit him soon to complete my pilgrimage, which was disrupted by certain troubles, notably the Armenian enemies who conspired against my nascent county."

After the departure of the messenger George, a candid dialogue unfolded between Count Baldwin of Boulogne and Lord Baldwin of Bourg. They both expressed their displeasure with George's praise for their rival Tancred's sacrifices. They feared that Tancred might seize Duke Godfrey's attention and take over the kingdom in the future, causing the Duke to forget about his brother, Count Baldwin of Boulogne, and his cousin, Lord Baldwin of Bourg.

Only six months had passed since the Crusaders took control of Jerusalem when a messenger from Prince

Bohemond arrived, inviting Count Baldwin of Boulogne to join him in a holy pilgrimage to the Sacred City. Prince Bohemond had returned to Antioch before the siege of Jerusalem in June 1099, following his dispute with Count Raymond IV of Toulouse over the governance of the city of Ma'arrat Nu'man, which they had wrested from the Muslims. Meanwhile, Count Baldwin of Boulogne had not contemplated joining the Crusaders marching to capture the Holy City.

The letter displayed a dubious kindness unprecedented from Bohemond to Baldwin of Boulogne, despite the rivalry that had arisen between Baldwin of Boulogne and Tancred, Bohemond's nephew, over Tarsus and Mamistra, as mentioned earlier. Nonetheless, Baldwin of Boulogne found himself compelled to agree to accompany his rival Bohemond on this visit to his brother Duke Godfrey, ruler of the Kingdom of Jerusalem. This decision aimed to dispel the accusations that had sullied his reputation for not being eager to fight Muslims and undertake the pilgrimage to the Promised Land.

Meanwhile, forces from Italy, particularly Tuscany, arrived in the East, accompanied by Archbishop Daimbert of Pisa. He would soon be appointed as the Patriarch of Jerusalem by the new Pope Paschal II, who succeeded Pope Urban II. Worth noting is that Pope Urban II passed away days after the Crusaders captured Jerusalem, although the news did not reach him. He died two weeks after the Crusaders accomplished their goal of capturing the Holy Sepulchre of Christ in Jerusalem (within the Church of the Resurrection).

The Italian forces joined the ranks of both Count Baldwin of Boulogne and Prince Bohemond. When they visited the

Holy City after a few weeks, their combined forces numbered over fifteen thousand fighters.

As these significant forces reached the Holy City, Duke Godfrey welcomed them warmly, along with their two Crusader leaders who had not taken part in the conquest of Jerusalem. Learning that his brother, Duke Godfrey, had granted his rival Tancred the province of Galilee as his fiefdom, Baldwin of Boulogne's spirits dampened, and his face darkened with anger, almost revealing his fury at this decision. However, he quickly recalled his previous attempt to win his brother's favor in his dispute with Tancred over Tarsus and Mamistra, which had failed miserably. Accompanying Bohemond, Tancred's uncle, he did not want to sour the mood of their sacred pilgrimage.

A month had passed since this visit, and everyone was celebrating Daimbert's inauguration as Patriarch of Jerusalem in the Church of the Resurrection. This inauguration had been orchestrated by Bohemond and Duke Godfrey, out of concern that Pope Paschal II would appoint a more compliant patriarch to the Holy City. Nevertheless, Daimbert demonstrated that he would not be a puppet in Duke Godfrey's hands. Several months later, he compelled Duke Godfrey to agree that if he died without an heir from his lineage, the kingdom would be handed over to the patriarch himself. This way, the clergy would be able to wrest the Kingdom of the Lord from the secular powers that had monopolized its rule since Duke Godfrey's installation as its ruler, under the title "Protector of the Holy Sepulchre."

The news reached Edessa, and this dialogue ensues between Count Baldwin of Boulogne and his cousin, Lord Baldwin of Bourg.

Lord Baldwin of Bourg: "Our worst fears have come true. Our lord Duke Godfrey has bowed down to Patriarch Daimbert, as if Daimbert were his savior. The crowning of that pompous and ungrateful Patriarch was thanks to the collaboration of our lord the Duke with Bohemond."

Count Baldwin of Boulogne: "I have already told you how weak my brother, the Duke, is under stress. He did not proclaim himself as the King of Jerusalem but settled for the title 'Guardian of the Holy Sepulcher,' as if he were too meek to merit the honor of ruling the kingdom. If only it were me in his shoes, I would show you how I would handle that arrogant Patriarch."

Lord Baldwin of Bourg: "I wish I were with our lord Duke Godfrey to stand by his side and hinder him from yielding. It seems that Tancred, the reckless, was useless as a counselor to the Duke. He did not lift a finger or even advise the Duke against conceding to that haughty Patriarch."

On the eighteenth of July in 1100 AD, and after a short span of no longer than two months from the Duke's abdication of the rule, he suddenly passed away.

The secular leaders in Jerusalem resolved to appoint his younger brother Count Baldwin of Boulogne – the current Count of Edessa – as their King since he was in the East, while his elder brother Count Eustace was residing in his fiefdom far away in France after he finished his pilgrimage and took part in the pillaging of Jerusalem two years ago.

Upon hearing the news, Patriarch Daimbert – the Patriarch of Jerusalem – hastened to send an urgent message to Bohemond – the Prince of Antioch – inviting him to seize the kingdom and urging him to speed up before the arrival of Count Baldwin of Boulogne.

However, Bohemond was occupied at that time with a different matter. He had received a letter from Gabriel the Armenian – the lord of Malatya – inviting him to seize Malatya and for him, i.e. Gabriel, to become his vassal. Gabriel also proposed that he would marry him daughter Morphia. Thus, Bohemond departed with a small force to seize Malatya, but he was ambushed by Muslim forces led by Gazi Gümüshtigin – the Ruler of the Sivas – and Bohemond fell captive into his grasp.

Therefore, when the Patriarch's envoy arrived at Antioch, he did not find Bohemond, nor did he find Tancred, who might have been on his way to Antioch when he heard the news of his uncle Bohemond's capture while he was in his fiefdom in Galilee, Palestine. Perhaps Tancred reached Antioch shortly after the Patriarch's envoy's arrival.

As for Count Baldwin of Boulogne, he safely arrived in Jerusalem with his forces in a swift and cautious journey. He had to traverse the Principality of Antioch on his way to Jerusalem, which was in the hands of his opponents, the Normans.

When Count Baldwin of Boulogne arrived with his forces in Jerusalem, he received a grand welcome from the secular leaders, while Patriarch Daimbert and the clergy subsided. The Patriarch sought asylum in one of the monasteries where he remained.

The Patriarch's avoidance of Count Baldwin of Boulogne and his refusal to greet or bless him as the ruler of the kingdom did not concern Count Baldwin. He spent five months ruling the kingdom by fait accompli, without being formally crowned as king. This continued until December of 1101 AD when he was crowned by the hand of the Patriarch himself, who had suffered under Baldwin's rule.

With this coronation, Baldwin of Boulogne became the first Crusader King of Jerusalem, known as the "Latin Kingdom of Jerusalem." The new king rewarded his former county, Edessa, to his cousin Lord Baldwin of Bourg as a token of appreciation for standing by his side in ruling the kingdom.

This dialogue unfolds between the new king, Baldwin of Boulogne, and the new count, Baldwin of Bourg.

King Baldwin of Boulogne: "You have finally achieved your esteemed goal and risen to the rank of count by my grace."

Count Baldwin of Bourg: "Indeed, my lord and patron. I am your faithful and devoted servant."

King Baldwin of Boulogne: "Our sincere collaboration seems to have borne the desired fruit, causing even the rebellious clergy to yield to the majority who proclaimed me as their king. These rebels have certainly learned their lesson, especially their leader Daimbert, who nearly handed my brother Godfrey's kingdom to our adversary Bohemond, whom I hope spends the rest of his life in Muslim captivity."

Count Baldwin of Bourg: "I thank God that he has fallen into the hands of the Muslims. However, Tancred, who has taken control of Antioch, is far more cunning than his uncle Bohemond, who was openly hostile. Tancred is a sly fox and cannot be trusted."

King Baldwin of Boulogne: "I hope you can find the right approach to manage him and thwart his schemes. He might conspire against us with our Muslim adversaries. This fox must be handled with the utmost care."

Count Baldwin of Bourg: "Yes, Your Majesty. We must collaborate for our own benefit and strengthen our authority in these unsettled lands. The kingdom still possesses only one seaport, Jaffa, since its establishment almost two years ago. Therefore, expansion and fortification are imperative. The former duke was preoccupied with his conflicts with the clergy, particularly the infamous Daimbert, and neglected to fortify the Holy Land."

King Baldwin of Boulogne: "Indeed, we must combine our efforts to secure the Holy Land, which faces threats from every direction, most notably from the rulers of Egypt—the Fatimids. They still control most of the eastern coast of the Levant, except for Jaffa, which fell under our control prior to our conquest of the Holy City. As for Tripoli and its territories, they were captured by the Shiite family of Banu Ammar, following a different doctrine from the Egyptian Fatimids, the Ismailis. They maintaine their independence along the coast, obstructing the expansion of the Kingdom of God. Meanwhile, their rivals, the Turks—the Seljuks—have declared their independence in the kingdoms of Aleppo to the north and Damascus to the south."

Count Baldwin of Bourg: "It appears that the rulers of Damascus, particularly their leader Toghtekin, who follows the Sunni doctrine, are cooperating with the Fatimid rulers of

Egypt despite their adherence to different doctrine. We will strive to shatter their alliance and disperse their ranks. This will make it easier for us to expand along the Syrian coast and annex the region to our kingdom. The security of the kingdom will remain uncertain until we liberate the entire coast from the Muslims, Turks, and Egypt's Fatimids alike. They all stand as adversaries to the kingdom of God."

King Baldwin of Boulogne: "Be as cautious with your county as you are with your sons, for we have sacrificed everything to establish it."

Count Baldwin of Bourg: "Do not underestimate my caution regarding this county. I am more guarded with it than I am with my sons who are yet to be born."

King Baldwin of Boulogne: "I hope that you will wed soon, so you can secure the future of your county for your sons and the people of Lorraine. Otherwise, our enemies, the southern Normans or others, might seize it."

Count Baldwin of Bourg: "I will take this matter seriously, for I am deeply committed to our rule and the Kingdom of God, which has come to establish justice and thwart cruelty and corruption."

King Baldwin of Boulogne: "I strongly recommend that you consider marrying Armenians. Winning them over is vital. We have suffered losses by alienating them when we confiscated their wealth and extorted them a few months ago. Your county cannot prosper or endure unless you incorporate them as citizens and Latin soldiers. They are a valuable asset, especially given that your county falls within the Armenian sphere of influence. We have had to engage with them ever since arriving in the East."

Count Baldwin of Bourg: "I have heard that Gabriel, Lord of Malatya, had offered his daughter Morphia to Bohemond for marriage. However, Bohemond has been captured by our enemies. I shall endeavor to persuade him to grant me his daughter's hand, particularly as I have heard of her remarkable beauty."

King Baldwin of Boulogne: "Indeed, selecting women seems to be your specialty. Perhaps Gabriel will even offer you the fortress of Malatya as a prize for this union."

Count Baldwin of Bourg: "I humbly seek your permission to depart in order to attend to matters in my county, Edessa, on your behalf. I aim to demonstrate my sincerity and loyalty to Your Majesty."

King Baldwin of Boulogne: "You have my permission to leave. May you be under God's protection."

Count Baldwin of Bourg returns to his county of Edessa, where his arrival is celebrated by his Crusader subjects, while the Armenian nobles shun his reception. The Count invites the very same Armenian nobles he extorted a few months ago to his council. He praises them highly, promising a new era in which no distinction exists between the Latins and the Armenians. He also shares his intention to marry into their community as a gesture of sincere cooperation.

One of the Armenian noblemen suggests that the Count marry the daughter of Gabriel the Armenian, Lord of Malatya. The Count enthusiastically endorses this proposal and entrusts the nobleman with the task of proposing the marriage to Gabriel's daughter, Morphia. Without hesitation, Gabriel agrees to the union between his daughter and Baldwin of Bourg.

A grand ceremony is held to celebrate this marriage – an event unparalleled in the city of Edessa since the establishment of the Crusader county two years prior. During this event, unprecedented harmony and friendliness prevail between the Latins and the Armenians.

Thus begins a new chapter in the relationship between the Latins, represented by Count Baldwin of Bourg, and the Armenians, represented by Gabriel. This political alliance marks the formation of a new partnership, with far-reaching consequences for the Crusader presence in the East. The marriage also provides an opportunity for the Armenians to involve themselves in the affairs of the Kingdom of Jerusalem through this alliance. The subsequent events that unfold over the next fifty years will attest to the significance of this alliance and its impact on the region.

A dialogue unfolds between Count Baldwin of Bourg and his wife, Countess Morphia, the daughter of Gabriel the Armenian.

The Count addresses his shy bride: "How beautiful is this moment, with your radiance illuminating our county and its gems sparkling in response."

Countess Morphia responds: "Thank you, my lord, for these kind words. It is I who is fortunate to have been blessed with the bravest and most gracefully poised among the Franks as my husband—a descendant of the illustrious family that reigns over the great Kingdom of France."

Count Baldwin of Bourg remarks: "I hope that our marriage will serve as an opportunity for understanding and cooperation between brethren of one faith, united by their love for God and their aversion to God's enemies—the pagan Muslims."

Countess Morphia adds: "I hope that we can refrain from turning this beautiful night into a rigid political discourse that detracts from its charm."

Count Baldwin of Bourg agrees: "You are right, my dear. These are indeed precious moments, and I hope that nothing will tarnish them."

Not long after these events, word came of a new Crusade summoned by Pope Paschal II to aid the first holy war declared by the departed Pope Urban II. This new Crusade drew mostly Italians from Lombardy in the north and Normans from the south, led by Raymond IV of Toulouse, who had his own agenda but would fail to fulfill it. The Italians aimed for Niksar, a city located in northeastern Anatolia, an area inhabited by a Muslim majority and the capital of the Danishmendids Muslims. Their goal was to free their lord Bohemond, who was held captive there, but they suffered great losses at the hands of the Turks under Gazi Gümüshtigin leadership. As a result, the Crusaders missed a significant opportunity that they could have taken advantage of to expand their domains in the East. Interestingly, King Baldwin I and Count Baldwin of Bourg did not join this new Crusade.

A conversation between Count Baldwin of Bourg and his wife, Countess Morphia, takes place after the failure of that campaign.

Countess Morphia: "The news of our brothers' defeats in Anatolia has filled my heart with sorrow and grief. I had hoped for their triumph over the foes who have plundered our land since five centuries."

Count Baldwin of Bourg: "Do you truly believe that the success of this campaign would have been in the best interests of your people, the Armenians? Can you imagine that Count Raymond, the traitor, would not pose a threat to our county once he establishes his own kingdom in the East? He has a history of siding with our enemies, the Byzantines, and their leader Alexios I Komnenos, who fancies himself the emperor of the Romans."

Countess Morphia: "I find myself perplexed by your envy of Count Raymond. I thought you appreciated his efforts and battles against our enemies, especially during the prolonged sieges of Antioch alongside his brother Bohemond, and the eventual liberation of Jerusalem."

Count Baldwin of Bourg: "There is no denying the efforts of Raymond and Bohemond, who nearly became your groom had fate not united us."

Here, Morphia smiles with a mysterious smile, as if she is saying, "I wish I had become a spouse to him, for he is handsome, courageous, and holds more power and reputation than you."

Baldwin of Bourg continues: "But Raymond has revealed his true colors by aligning with the Roman emperor instead of showing loyalty to our lord, the King of France, and his fellow Crusaders. He has forsaken the noble cause of the Crusade for his allegiance to our Greek adversaries."

Countess Morphia: "It appears that conflicts from the West have found their way into your 'divine' project initiated by the Western Church six years ago."

Count Baldwin of Bourg catches himself, fearing that his Armenian wife might discover the depth of disagreements among the Crusader leaders. He responds: "Indeed, my lady. Disputes persist in the West, but most of us have united under this divine project, sacrificing everything to aid our Eastern brethren and your people, the Armenians. Yet, some, like Raymond, remain ambiguous in their intentions."

Countess Morphia: "May your hearts heal, leaving behind pain and resentment. Let love and harmony prevail once more, as unity and cooperation are paramount in our struggle against our Muslim adversaries, who aim to divide us despite our unity with this marriage."

Count Baldwin of Bourg: "Indeed, the sacred bond that unites me with the most beautiful woman in this blessed land, the land of our forefathers and apostles."

Countess Morphia: "I pray that God blesses us with a son to bring joy to our lives, strengthen our enduring county, and defend it against our enemies, working in tandem with the kings of Jerusalem."

Count Baldwin of Bourg: "It seems my cousin, King Baldwin of Boulogne, may not have an heir, as he and Lady Erad have yet to bear a child since their marriage three years ago. Perhaps he will entrust me with the rule of the kingdom."

Countess Morphia: "May our lord king enjoy a long life, and may he consider you as his successor, preventing his brother Eustace or cousins from inheriting."

Count Baldwin of Bourg: "May God protect the kingdom and our lord King Baldwin of Boulogne, a man of virtue and rare character."

Countess Morphia: "I have heard rumors about the king's dissatisfaction with his wife and his questionable relationships with other women."

Count Baldwin of Bourg: "Disregard these rumors, my lady. They aim to stain the honor of Crusaders like us, who carry the cross for the salvation of our souls and the support of our Eastern brethren, including your people."

Countess Morphia: "I trust your words and your honorable character, as well as our lord's. Thank you, my dear."

For four blissful years, Baldwin of Bourg enjoyed the company of his wife, Morphia, who bore him three lovely daughters: Melisende, the eldest; then Alice; and Hodierna. Morphia raised them with care and wisdom, teaching them the importance of public affairs and cultivating in them a flair for leadership from a young age. She also instilled in them a sense of pride in their Armenian heritage and, perhaps, a desire to avenge the wrongs done by the Crusaders to their people. While the Crusaders claimed to be defenders of the Eastern Christians under Muslim rule, they often oppressed and exploited them. Historical sources are silent about the childhood of these girls, but it is clear that Morphia's influence was strong and lasting. She also softened the heart of her husband, who was known as a harsh and ruthless warrior. Baldwin grew more attached to Morphia and their daughters, finding in them a source of love and joy he had never experienced in his military life. Of all his children, Melisende was the closest to his heart, and she is the main character of our story.

In 1104, after four years of the capture of Bohemond, Prince of Antioch, by the Muslims, Baldwin of Bourg, then the Count of Edessa, wrote a letter to his cousin Baldwin of Boulogne, the King of Jerusalem, urging him to join in rescuing Bohemond. He warned him of the danger posed by Bohemond's regent, Tancred, who had taken over Antioch and expanded his domain into Cilicia in southern Anatolia near his county. He alerted him that Tancred had also seized the fortress of Apamea and the port of Latakia and that he would become too powerful and independent. Baldwin of Bourg also informed King Baldwin that he had secretly cooperated with the Patriarch of Antioch to release Bohemond by paying a ransom. The ransom was demanded by Gazi Gümüshtigin, the Ruler of the Danishmendids, who held Bohemond captive. Baldwin emphasized to his cousin that Tancred would not lift a finger to free his uncle because he wanted to rule Antioch himself.

The two leaders agreed to work together to free Bohemond, not out of love for him, but because they preferred him over Tancred, who was arrogant and reckless, and avoided by many. They managed to secure Bohemond's release, and he returned to Antioch, where he was warmly and gleefully greeted by his people and by Tancred. Tancred showed great joy at his uncle's release, even though he did not contribute a penny to his ransom. Bohemond thanked Tancred and expressed his gratitude for preserving his principality during the stressful period of his captivity, and for adding Latakia and Apamea to it.

This dialogue takes place between Baldwin of Bourg and his wife, Countess Morfia.

Countess Morphia: "I used to want to believe your words about the unity among the Crusaders, but today I have become convinced that the rift between you all is beyond repair. Even Tancred did not come to the aid of his own uncle, the one who has supported him, his lord, and benefactor."

Count Baldwin of Bourg: "Trust me, Tancred does not deserve to be called a true Crusader. He is simply selfish, concerned only with his own interests rather than the greater cause. I recognized his true nature when we disagreed about capturing the fortresses of Tarsus and Mamistra from the Muslims seven years ago in 1097."

Countess Morphia: "But there are others who tell a different tale from what you are saying. They paint Tancred as a victim of injustice and arrogance imposed by you and your cousin Baldwin of Boulogne. They claim you made him relinquish Tarsus and take down the Normandy flags he raised. Then, you pursued him to Mamistra, demanding his submission to your authority, which he refused, leading to a confrontation."

Count Baldwin of Bourg: "Do not be swayed by these rumors. It was Tancred who initiated the quarrel and created the problem, not me or my cousin King Baldwin of Boulogne."

Countess Morphia: "It seems you are always unwavering in your stance and quick to provide unreasonable justifications. You never seem to admit your mistakes, instead insisting you are always right and anyone who disagrees is wrong."

Count Baldwin of Bourg: "I envision a day when I am crowned king, a day when I can finally bring Tancred, that arrogant man, to heel. He will have to follow my commands then, and I will put an end to the ambitions of these prideful southern Normans."

Not a month had passed after the release of Bohemond when he received a covert message from Count Baldwin of Bourg, offering him an alliance for a joint campaign to conquer the Islamic fortress of Harran, located near the capital of the County of Edessa. In this message, Count Baldwin of Bourg reminded him of the efforts that had been made to secure his freedom. Bohemond had learned about the endeavors undertaken by Baldwin of Bourg and his cousin, King Baldwin of Boulogne, to secure his release. However, these efforts were not born out of affection for him but rather out of a desire to spite his nephew, Tancred, with whom they found it difficult to deal.

Carrying a sense of resentment and suspicion, Bohemond believed that it was King Baldwin of Boulogne who had abandoned him years ago to the Muslim Turks when he was the Count of Edessa. It was under his rule that he had been captured due to his movement with a small force to capture Malatya from Gabriel the Armenian. This event led to his subsequent captivity. With the intent to exact revenge upon King Baldwin of Boulogne, Bohemond saw an opportunity in the form of his cousin Baldwin of Bourg, who had taken over the County of Edessa after the former was crowned the King of Jerusalem four years prior. Thus, Bohemond readily agreed to the alliance without hesitation and proceeded to march his forces to join those of his ally, Baldwin of Bourg.

As Count Baldwin of Bourg prepares to set out with his troops for this mission, a dialogue unfolds between him and his cousin Lord Joscelin de Courtenay, who arrived two years ago in the county to be his partner in ruling it.

Joscelin de Courtenay: "I hope Bohemond and Tancred will finally be truthful this time. We have had our fill of their dishonesty."

Count Baldwin of Bourg: "I do not think Bohemond would be ungrateful enough to betray us and buy into the accusations of Tancred. After all, Tancred did nothing to secure his release."

Joscelin de Courtenay: "The southern Normans have repeatedly shown that they lack a moral code preventing them from abandoning their allies. Their pursuit of self-interest comes before considerations of the greater good or the sacred divine project."

Count Baldwin of Bourg: "I am optimistic that we can put the past behind us and rebuild our relationship with the southern Norman allies. Our sincerity, cooperation, and friendship might just help them maintain this alliance with us."

Joscelin de Courtenay: "True confirmation of this will come in a few days when we lay siege to Harran and capture it. I hope to witness the results of this alliance and the integrity of the southern Normans towards us."

The allied Crusader forces marched and laid siege to the fortress of Harran. The surrender of the fortress was delayed due to a dispute that arose between the two allied parties over who would rule the fortress. It is said that Baldwin of Bourg struck a deal with the Muslims defending the fortress, urging them to resist and not surrender until all the allied Crusader forces returned. He promised to return with his forces after their withdrawal and take control of the fortress for himself. However, Tancred intervened to thwart this plot. He incited his uncle Bohemond not to hand over the fortress to Baldwin of Bourg, the Count of Edessa, despite it being only eighty kilometers away from the city of Edessa.

Then, Muslim reinforcements arrived at Harran, catching the allied Crusaders by surprise. The Muslim forces were led by Sukman, the lord of Mardin, and Jikirmish, the governor of Mosul. When the Muslim forces clashed with the Crusader forces, the latter were quickly defeated, particularly Antioch's forces, even before the battle was decided. In fact, Bohemond and Tancred were among the first to flee. Count Baldwin of Bourg and his cousin Joscelin de Courtenay fell into Muslim captivity. This confirmed that the division among the Crusader leaders was too deep to be mended, not even after the four years Bohemond spent in Muslim captivity.

After the Count of Edessa, Baldwin of Bourg, and his right-hand man Joscelin de Courtenay were captured, Bohemond claimed the throne of the county. However, he grew restless in the East and sailed for his domain in Taranto, located in the south of Italy. He entrusted Tancred with the principality of Antioch and the county of Edessa. Subsequently, he joined forces with King Philip I of France in a new crusade, this time aimed against the Christian Byzantines, not the Muslims. A political and matrimonial arrangement was made between the French king and Bohemond. Bohemond married the King's daughter, Constance, while Tancred took the king's illegitimate daughter, Cecilia, as his bride.

Jikirmish, the governor of Mosul, showed mercy to his Crusader prisoners, keeping them together in one place. He hoped that the Crusader leaders would pay a substantial ransom for their release.

Four long years of captivity had passed, and now it was the year 1107 AD when this frank dialogue unfolds between the two Crusader prisoners, languishing in their chains.

Jocelyn de Courtenay: "We have been captives for so long, suffering and forgotten by our allies after they failed us in that ill-fated battle. I wish I could escape this prison and take revenge on those two traitors."

Count Baldwin of Bourg: "Yes, our captivity has been long, and we have been reduced to two birds with clipped wings, robbed of our freedom. Not even my cousin, King Baldwin of Boulogne, came to our rescue. I was blindsided by his betrayal, as if he had no recollection of my support when he was Count of Edessa, or when he took over the kingdom after the death of his brother Duke Godfrey seven years ago."

Jocelyn de Courtenay: "The world is closing in on us, and we have lost all hope in our brothers who have left us to rot in captivity. If it were not for the kindness of our captor, Jikirmish, we might have preferred death over spending our lives between these gloomy walls."

Count Baldwin of Bourg: "Never would I have expected that Jikirmish would seek to earn our trust and friendship, as if he had a vision of joining forces with us against our foes in the days to come. I have grown to feel a bond with him that rivals my connection with our brothers from the Crusaders, except for those who betrayed us, like the infamous turncoats Bohemond and Tancred."

Jocelyn de Courtenay: "I might have an idea to propose that could help toward our release on special terms, especially now that we have lost all hope in our brothers who have left us to suffer in captivity. I am thinking that we could offer Jikirmish my release first in exchange for hostages from our relatives, whom we would hand over to him. Then, after my release, I could arrange the ransom for both of us."

Count Baldwin of Bourg: "Yes, that is a fine plan, and I will personally present it to Lord Jikirmish soon. I will even suggest joining forces to fight all our enemies together, whether they be Crusaders or Muslims. Things have become blurred for me; I can no longer distinguish between my allies and enemies. I have given up on regaining my freedom after these four bleak years in captivity. I have been deprived of my three little ones, especially Hodierna, who was only one month old when I was captured. How I wish I could be out playing with Melisende, who is now six years old, and Alice, who is five."

When the governor of Mosul, Jikirmish, learned about Count Baldwin of Bourg's desire to meet him, he welcomed the idea, and the meeting took place secretly at Jikirmish's house. They agreed that Jocelyn de Courtenay would be released first, in exchange for Crusader hostages that he would hand over to Jikirmish. Jocelyn de Courtenay would then arrange the full ransom for the two prisoners. The ransom was set at twenty thousand Byzantine coins for each of them, which was a substantial sum at that time. Once the ransom was paid, Jikirmish would release the hostages and Baldwin of Bourg.

Count Baldwin of Bourg later learned that Jikirmish was in a tight spot, as Sultan Muhammad al-Saljuki was dissatisfied with him and determined to remove him from his position as the ruler of Mosul.

As events escalated, the Crusader hostages were delivered to Jikirmish, and Jocelyn was released. However, the hostages managed to escape from the Muslims. Consequently, Jocelyn de Courtenay gained his freedom without paying a ransom, while Baldwin of Bourg remained in captivity.

Jocelyn de Courtenay then marched with his Crusader and Armenian allies toward his fiefdom in Tell Bashir, aiming to reclaim it from the control of Tancred. Upon learning of Jocelyn de Courtenay's arrival alongside his forces, Richard, the Crusader ruler of Tell Bashir appointed by Tancred, fled to the city of Edessa and refused to surrender Edessa to Jocelyn de Courtenay. To counter Tancred's hold, Jocelyn de Courtenay allied with Armenians opposed to Tancred, led by Kogh Vasil, the lord of the fortress Kaysun.

In November of 1107 AD, Sultan Muhammad al-Saljuki ousted Jikirmish and appointed Jawali Saqawa as ruler over Mosul and Al-Jazira, instructing him to capture Mosul from Jikirmish. Jawali defeated Jikirmish's forces, captured Jikirmish himself, who died soon after in captivity. Jawali then took control of Mosul from Jikirmish's supporters. King Ridwan of Aleppo initially sided with the Sultan's campaign to support Jawali, but he later discovered Jawali's ambitions to make Ridwan the Sultan of all the Seljuks, replacing Sultan Muhammad al-Saljuki. He wanted to be the Atabeg (right hand) of Ridwan and control him as he wants. Thus, Ridwan distanced himself from Jawali.

After ruling Mosul, Jawali treated his captive, Count Baldwin of Bourg, kindly, in the hopes of forming an alliance. Jawali wanted to be the Atabeg of a weak Seljuk sultan, instead of the powerful Sultan Muhammad. One day, Jawali summoned Baldwin to a secret meeting, revealing that he had to leave Mosul because Sultan Muhammad al-Saljuki sent a large force to take the city from him. He proposed a plan where Baldwin and Jawali would work together to make Irtash, son of Sultan Tutush, the Sultan of the Seljuks, instead of Sultan Muhammad al-Saljuki. Their goal was to seize the Kingdom of Aleppo from its ruler, Ridwan. Irtash was a half-brother of King Ridwan.

A frank discussion unfolds between the governor of Mosul, Jawali Saqawa, and his Crusader captive, Count Baldwin of Bourg.

Count Baldwin of Bourg: "It seems to me, my lord, that the conflicts among your people are as intense as ours among the Crusaders. Everyone seems to crave power, even if it means betraying their own, and they are willing to form alliances with those of different faiths when it serves their interests."

Jawali Saqawa: "Indeed, the conflicts among us Muslim leaders are profound and often personal, much like yours. You were betrayed by your ally, Bohemond, who pretended to put aside his rivalry with you, just as my loyalty to Sultan Muhammad was met with ingratitude and mistrust. When Sadaqa bin Mazid, the lord of Al-Hilla in southern Iraq, rose against him a few months ago, my hesitation to send troops to aid him was seen as defiance."

Count Baldwin of Bourg: "My lord, could you please update me on recent events in my county? I haven't heard anything since my cousin Joscelin de Courtenay was released from imprisonment and reclaimed his capital, Tell Bashir, from Tancred's control over a year ago. I'm also worried about my daughters, Melisende, Alice, and Hodierna. They have been separated from their dear father for far too long."

Jawali Saqawa: "Your daughters have moved with their grandfather, Gabriel, and their mother since Tancred took control of your county. Lady Morphia refused to stay in Edessa under Tancred's rule, and his deputy, the wicked Richard, oppressed the Armenian population in your county and seized their property."

Count Baldwin of Bourg: "How I have missed my dear daughters! I long to see Melisende and look into her sparkling eyes, full of love and hope. When I last saw her, she was just four years old. I miss Alice's stubbornness, always refusing to share her toys with her sister Melisende. As for Hodierna, I barely had the chance to see her; she was only a month old when I was captured. I have so much lost time to make up for. Can you imagine how much I have missed my little ones? I even miss them more than I miss their mother."

Jawali Saqawa: "The animosity between your cousin Joscelin de Courtenay and Tancred remains intense. Joscelin formed an alliance with the Armenian commander Kogh Vasil of Kaysum but couldn't persuade Tancred to relinquish control of Edessa to your county. As for Bohemond, he waged a holy war against the Byzantines and suffered a devastating defeat at the hands of Byzantine Emperor Alexios Komnenos in the Balkans a few months ago. He signed a treaty with the emperor, pledging to return the city of Antioch, but Tancred still refuses to yield control of Edessa to the Byzantines."

Count Baldwin of Bourg: "I thank God that I have seen my enemy Bohemond humbled, and I pray to the Almighty to bring about Tancred's downfall. These people claim to be on a holy mission in the East, but their actions often serve their personal interests. Bohemond exploited Pope Paschal II's naivety in declaring a holy war against the Christian Byzantines, even though he had previously fought against your people in a crusade. They all seem to manipulate religion for their own gain and declare their wars as holy."

Jawali Saqawa: "All of that is now beside the point. Our primary goal is to forge a sacred alliance that unites us to achieve our noble objectives. I aim to control the Seljuk state by supporting the inexperienced Irtash as Sultan and then assume the position of Atabeg and right hand. Sultan Muhammad al-Seljuki ousted me from Mosul and sent Mawdud to rule in my place and capture me."

Count Baldwin of Bourg: "You appear to be a skilled politician, and I pledge my loyalty to you. You can trust in my sincerity regarding our alliance, even if you were to release me right now without any hostages, waiting for my ransom to be paid."

Jawali took Count Baldwin of Bourg's hand, and together they swore loyalty in a sacred alliance against their common enemies, whether Muslim or Crusader. Jawali attempted to garner support from other Muslims for his project, including Ilghazi, the lord of Mardin, who had rebelled against Sultan Muhammad al-Seljuki. Unfortunately, he failed in this endeavor. However, he did manage to win over Badran and

Mansur, the sons of Sadaqa ibn Mazid, the lord of al-Al-Hilla in southern Iraq, who had been killed by Sultan Muhammad al-Seljuki a few months prior.

On the other side, King Ridwan learned of Jawali's intentions to seize Aleppo and take control of the Seljuk sultanate from Sultan Muhammad al-Seljuki. In response, he reluctantly sought an alliance with his Crusader enemy, Tancred, who had already seized most of his lands, leaving him with only a few forts near his capital, Aleppo.

This alliance between Count Baldwin of Bourg and Jawali was arranged by Salim ibn Malik, the Muslim lord of Ja'bar Castle, who had a positive relationship with the Crusaders of Edessa. Meanwhile, Tancred, the Crusader, accepted an alliance with his enemy, King Ridwan, the Muslim. Ridwan sent six hundred knights to join Tancred's forces, while Jawali's ally, Count Baldwin of Bourg, his cousin Jocelin de Courtenay, and Kogh Vasil, the Armenian lord of Kaysum, joined Jawali's alliance.

In the end, Tancred and Ridwan's alliance defeated Jawali and his allies in a short battle at Jubba, near Tell Bashir, in October 1108 AD. Jawali's master plan to control the Muslim Seljuk sultanate failed. However, Count Baldwin of Bourg's plan to regain his capital city, Edessa, finally succeeded with the intervention of King Baldwin of Boulogne, who mediated the resolution of their longstanding dispute. The alliance between Tancred and Ridwan dissolved as quickly as it had formed, and their enmity returned a few months after the Jubba incident.

After his defeat, Jawali sought forgiveness from Sultan Muhammad al-Seljuki, who pardoned him. With this, things settled in favor of Count Baldwin of Bourg, and his county returned to its unity under his rule.

Count Baldwin of Bourg then traveled to the stronghold of Malatya to reunite with his family. He was overjoyed to see his daughters, especially Melisende, who was now eight years old and had grown more aware of her surroundings. The Count expressed his yearning for his wife, Morphia, who was ecstatic about his release after their long separation.

Gabriel the Armenian, Morphia's father, appeared delighted to see his son-in-law released. He was elated he could be finally free from Tancred's rule, who had oppressed him when he became the ruler of the county of Edessa, including Malatya, which Gabriel had governed as a deputy for Count Baldwin of Bourg before his capture. Count Baldwin of Bourg perceived that Gabriel's reluctance to pay his ransom was a form of betrayal. Then the Count returned with his family to his county, where the family was reunited once again, and the Count's authority over the county and the rest of the county was restored after the intervention of King Baldwin of Boulogne.

After a few months, the Count visited Gabriel in Malatya without his family, and he extorted his father in law. The Count claimed that his soldiers would shave his beard if he didn't pay their overdue wages, which had been accumulating for months. This act was considered a great insult to the Easterners at the time. Therefore, Gabriel pretended to believe it and agreed to pay the Crusader soldiers their overdue wages to prevent his son-in-law from being disgraced in front of him. The amount was a significant sum of twenty thousand gold pieces Michaelian. When the Count returned happily to

Edessa with the money, his wife, Countess Morphia, learned of the extortion and was furious with her husband.

A heated argument ensues between Morphia and her husband the Count.

Countess Morphia: "I never expected you to treat my father with such disdain. He sacrificed everything for the sake of God, giving you his only fortress, Malatya, and marrying you to his most cherished daughter, all for the Cross and the Crusaders."

Count Baldwin of Bourg: "My dear, I believe there's a misunderstanding. I didn't extort your father; I did it to pay my soldiers who haven't received wages in six months. I will never forget the favors your father bestowed upon me, offering his only fortress and the hand of his beautiful and wise daughter."

Countess Morphia: "Your actions make it seem like you mistrust me and my Armenian people, as if we were your enemies. We share the same faith and should be united by our belief in Christ."

Count Baldwin of Bourg: "Please understand, my love, the toll four long years in captivity took on me, not to mention the betrayal of Bohemond and Tancred. I felt abandoned by everyone, as if I didn't belong."

Countess Morphia: "You claim my father didn't do his best to release you, but ransoming captive Crusader leaders isn't his responsibility. Four years ago, Kogh Vasil, the Armenian lord of Kaysum, helped Bohemond's release, even though he was abandoned by Tancred. Bohemond didn't blame Tancred. But here you are today, blaming my father for not rushing to your rescue. It is strange how Crusaders expect Armenians to pay ransoms after confiscating their money, as your cousin Baldwin of Boulogne did more than nine years ago when he was the Count of Edessa."

Count Baldwin of Bourg: "Forgive me, my dear. I believe you're being too harsh in your criticism of how your people were treated. I didn't urge my cousin King Baldwin of Boulogne to do that, and I have cooperated sincerely with your Armenian people. My actions should attest to that. We're connected by the sacred bond of marriage, a bond I hope will last forever. I have grown fond of you and your people who have supported the divine Crusader project. I apologize for my improper behavior toward your dear father."

Countess Morphia: "I appreciate your apology and your respect and loyalty to your Armenian brothers, especially my father."

When the storm of disagreement between them subsided, Melisende entered with her bright face, smiling at her parents and joking with them after their recent disagreement. Her father hugged her tightly against his chest and playfully addressed her mother, saying: "No matter how much we differ, we will never reach the point of separation, for this beautiful sun and her sisters, Alice and Hodierna, are a beacon lighting the way to our enduring and steadfast love."

Two years after his release, Baldwin of Bourg had firmly established his rule over Edessa County. However, a massive Muslim offensive threatened to disrupt this peace. A major campaign led by Seljuk Sultan Muhammad and his Mosul governor, Sharaf al-Din Mawdud, set off to lay a fierce siege on the city of Edessa in 1110 AD. They were joined by several other Muslim leaders, including Tughtakin of Damascus, who proved his loyalty to Mawdud.

These large armed forces imposed a severe siege on the city of Edessa. Baldwin of Bourg did his utmost to reinforce the city's defenses and sent urgent pleas for help to his cousin, King Baldwin of Jerusalem, and to his rival, Tancred, who was then acting as regent for the young Prince Bohemond II in southern Italy. It is worth noting that Tancred had ruled Antioch as regent for Bohemond II after the death of Bohemond I in Italy a few months earlier. He would remain in this role for two more years while Bohemond II was under the custody of his uncle William, the Count of Apulia, who feared that Tancred might conspire to harm him.

When Mawdud learned of the arrival of the Crusader forces led by the King of Jerusalem to aid Edessa, he lifted the siege and moved east across the Euphrates to Harran, hoping to lure the Crusaders into an open battle where they would be outnumbered. The Crusaders, however, marched to Edessa, supplied it with aid, and then left the city before the Muslim forces returned to besiege it again. The Crusaders should have stayed and defended Edessa vigorously, but they crossed the Euphrates heading west, with even the Count of Edessa himself leaving his city with the Crusader forces. The Count of Edessa left the county to the Armenian all alone, who demonstrated their steadfastness despite their small number and vulnerability. The Crusaders, including Baldwin of Bourg, appeared to devalue the city. Historical sources do not mention any efforts by the Crusaders to cut off the Muslim forces' supplies during the siege to force them to lift it.

Simultaneously, the Muslim forces were disunited and lacked unified command. Consequently, many of them left the siege without obtaining permission from their leader, Mawdud. This compelled Mawdud to lift the siege on the city, and it was saved, thanks to God's grace and the resilience of its Armenian inhabitants. Baldwin of Bourg returned joyfully to his beloved capital, acting as if he had sacrificed everything dear to him for the sanctity and independence of the city.

A heated argument takes place between Count Baldwin of Bourg and his wife Countess Morphia one day after his return to his capital.

Countess Morphia: "Your commitment to the independence of our capital, my lord, is truly commendable. Your followers and Crusader allies have shown unwavering dedication to their holy cause."

Count Baldwin of Bourg: "I appreciate your words, my lady. However, I sense some sarcasm in your compliment. Are you suggesting that my decision to leave the city with our forces heading west of the Euphrates was cowardly? Let me clarify that our plan was to head south first and strike at the city of Damascus, where Tughtekin, who had joined the Muslim campaign, would be forced to withdraw to defend his capital. This would compel the Muslim forces led by Mawdud to lift the siege on our capital. I'm grateful that God preserved this holy city, the first city to convert to Christianity at the beginning of the fourth century, even preceding the conversion of the Roman Emperor Constantine the Great in 312 AD, during the rule of your ancestors, the faithful Armenians."

Countess Morphia: "It appears you are more of a historian than a political and military leader. But let us not digress. I have never considered you a coward who would abandon your city and leave it in the hands of our Armenian brethren, whom you describe as weak. The audacity of you claiming heroism, and describing your cowardly escape as a strategic plan is beyond the realm of words!"

Count Baldwin of Bourg: "Please, my lady, military matters are not within your domain. Your lack of experience and knowledge in siege warfare and military strategies is evident. We lacked the necessary strength to face the overwhelming Muslim campaign head-on, which is why we fortified ourselves within the strong city of Edessa. Going east of the Euphrates into enemy-controlled territory with our small forces would have meant certain defeat. We would have been outnumbered and outmatched, falling into the trap of the Muslim forces."

Countess Morphia: "I hope I won't regret trusting in your commitment to the divine cause."

Count Baldwin of Bourg: "Time and actions will demonstrate my dedication to the divine Crusader cause, especially if I have to assume the rule of the Kingdom of Jerusalem in the absence of my cousin Baldwin of Boulogne, who has no heir in the East but me."

Countess Morphia: "I doubt that a man who fled his capital and left it in the hands of his Latin people to an uncertain fate is fit to rule the Kingdom of God. Such moral principles are not befitting a ruler."

Count Baldwin of Bourg: "Do you believe that my cousin, the King of Jerusalem, is a better leader or more courageous than I am? Let us not forget that he conspired against your people and even committed treachery by killing his adoptive father, Prince Thoros, while he…"

Countess Morphia: "It seems you are now willing to reveal your cousin's secrets, despite having always spoken highly of him."

Count Baldwin of Bourg: "My intention was not to disrespect His Majesty's dignity or reputation. I remain a loyal follower of his."

Countess Morphia: "Indeed, a loyal follower you are!"

Count Baldwin of Bourg: "My lady, I humbly request that you refrain from involving yourself in political matters. Focus on your family responsibilities and the upbringing of our daughters, especially Melisende, who will one day rule Edessa and possibly even Jerusalem. If only we had a son to inherit our kingdom."

Countess Morphia: "You need not worry about their upbringing. I am fully committed to instilling in them values of loyalty, virtue, compassion, and devotion to the holy cause. Let us pray that God blesses us with a son who can carry on our legacy and inherit our kingdom."

Count Baldwin of Bourg: "You are a wonderful mother, my love. Your care during my wretched captivity has been evident in our daughters' affection and reverence for me."

Countess Morphia: "I simply fulfill my duty to God and His holy cause through my service and commitment."

Two years after this incident, in 1112 AD, Tancred passed away, entrusting his cousin, Roger of Salerno, with the responsibility of governing the Principality of Antioch as regent for Bohemond II, the son of Bohemond I. Bohemond I had passed away in 1109 AD in his fiefdom in southern Italy while preparing for a new crusade against the Byzantine Empire, seeking to avenge the defeat he had suffered at the hands of the Byzantine Emperor Alexios Komnenos a year earlier in the Balkans. His son, Bohemond II, who was only two years old at the time, became his successor. He remained in southern Italy with his uncle William, the ruler of Apulia. By this time, he had reached the age of five but had not yet journeyed to Antioch which was being usurped by Tancred as regent for Bohemond II. This delay was due to his uncle William's concerns that Tancred might have sinister intentions. Ironically, upon hearing of Tancred's death, Count Baldwin of Bourg expressed deep sorrow, despite his longstanding animosity toward him.

The following conversation takes place between Count Baldwin of Bourg and his wife, Countess Morphia.

Countess Morphia: "You are quite the actor, my lord. You pretend to mourn your enemy Tancred as if he were your friend."

Count Baldwin of Bourg: "I despised him while he was alive, but now I recognize his value. His state is in peril, for his heir lacks the valor and strength he possessed."

Countess Morphia: "You have never shown much interest in the affairs of Antioch or any other domain of the Crusader lords."

Count Baldwin of Bourg: "I have a vision for the future, my lady. Perhaps soon, I will become the King of Jerusalem, for my cousin King Baldwin of Boulogne has no son to inherit his crown. The Crusader states in the East will pledge true allegiance to me, unlike the current situation with my feeble cousin Baldwin of Boulogne. I will take steps to establish the true supremacy of the Kingdom of God. I plan to begin by befriending Roger, the guardian of Bohemond II, and offering him my sister's hand in marriage. Additionally, I will arrange a marriage between Bohemond II and one of my daughters when he comes of age. This way, I can easily exert control when he assumes rule in Antioch."

Countess Morphia: "You paint a vivid picture of the future, as if you have already become the king who commands the obedience of all and masterfully rules the Kingdom of God, bending the wills of the Crusaders in the East to your own."

A conflict erupted between Count Baldwin of Bourg and his cousin, Lord Joscelin de Courtenay, at the end of 1113 AD. Count Baldwin had shared governance of the county with Joscelin since 1102 AD, granting him lands west of the Euphrates River, including fortresses like Tell Basher, Qura-Dalouk-Ein Tab, and Ra'wandan. The tension between them reached a breaking point when the Count compelled Joscelin to relinquish all the lands he had previously granted him and forced him to leave the county. Joscelin departed with a heavy heart and sought refuge with King Baldwin of Boulogne, who consoled him and appointed him to govern the region of Galilee and Tiberias in Palestine.

This dialogue unfolds between Count Baldwin of Bourg and his wife, Countess Morphia, regarding the matter of Joscelin de Courtenay.

Countess Morphia: "You Crusaders have no mercy for your Armenian kin, and you squeeze them dry. That's a fact I have come to terms with. But now you have revealed how much you begrudge each other. Envy has clouded your vision, leading you to accuse your faithful ally of defying your power and blaming him for taking the rich fiefs, while you hold the poor ones. Yet, it was you who willingly granted Joscelin de Courtenay these fiefs, and they are not even under his own possession. He is still your vassal, and he has never committed any act of insubordination. Have you forgotten that he was your fellow prisoner for three years, even sacrificing himself voluntarily as a hostage to free you? Have you ever witnessed such devotion from any other man?"

Count Baldwin of Bourg: "Yes, I cannot deny that Joscelin de Courtenay was loyal and true to me, and that he put his life at stake for me. However, recently, some of his men have been acting in a way that shows disobedience to my authority."

Countess Morphia: "Have you verified these actions and questioned Joscelin de Courtenay about them, or have you made a hasty verdict based on the deeds of some of his men, as if you were looking for any pretext to dispose of him? He is your right arm in governing the county."

Count Baldwin of Bourg: "I implore you not to meddle in my decisions, for I always act for the benefit of the county."

Countess Morphia: "You always act for your own benefit, placing it before the benefit of the county. It is in the county's best interest that you retain Joscelin de Courtenay by your side to assist you against the perils that besiege us from all sides."

Count Baldwin of Bourg: "You may have some reason in your perspective, but I am resolved not to withdraw from this decision, so as not to appear uncertain in my judgment in the eyes of my soldiers."

Countess Morphia: "Perhaps a day will come when you will need the aid of Joscelin de Courtenay, especially when your cousin the King passes away without an heir. Then, you will have to seek the help of the one who suffered this grave injustice."

Count Baldwin of Bourg: "Please do not interfere in my choices, for I am assured of their soundness, and I am following the right path."

Countess Morphia: "Time will reveal whose path is the right one."

Weeks go by, then news arrives from the Kingdom of Jerusalem. The King has undertaken a bizarre venture, where he claimed that he divorced his Armenian wife Erd, daughter of Thoros, and married the Countess of Sicily, mother of King Roger II, son of Roger I, named Adelaide.

Upon hearing the news, this discussion takes place between Count Baldwin of Bourg and his wife, Countess Morphia.

Countess Morphia: "Can you believe the latest news about your cousin? He is still married to Erda and has now married another woman. It is like he has forgotten our religious teachings that forbid polygamy."

Count Baldwin of Bourg: "You're absolutely right, my dear. This time, my cousin has really gone too far, all because of that religious adviser, Arnulf, from the Church of the Resurrection. He is leading him astray with these ideas, including polygamy. To think the King is following his advice after narrowly escaping death a few weeks ago! He was defeated by the forces of Mawdud, the governor of Mosul, and his ally, the prince of Damascus Tughtakin, near Tiberias. He was almost taken prisoner, but he found refuge in one of the nearby mountains that protected him from the attack of the

Muslim forces. He received help from Roger son of Richard, the guardian of the state of Antioch, and the forces of Count Tripoli Pons son of Bertrand son of Raymond."

Countess Morphia: "I can't help but wonder if you're worried about losing your chance to rule the kingdom if the King has a son with Countess Adelaide. I heard that Baldwin of Boulogne plans to cede the Kingdom of God to King Roger II's son if he doesn't have a son of his own."

Count Baldwin of Bourg: "Yes, I am concerned about the kingdom's future and the consequences of ignoring our religious laws against polygamy. If this pledge from King Baldwin of Boulogne is true to cede to Roger, then the Kingdom of God will be lost to the wicked southern Normans, relatives of Bohemond and Tancred the traitors."

Countess Morphia: "Yes, my lord, I share your fear, my lord, that you will lose the Kingdom of God to your Norman rivals, but if it were to come to you, then the kingdom would be safe and sound and in God's care."

Count Baldwin of Bourg: "We are more worthy than anyone else to cling to our religion, for we have forsaken everything we own and embarked on this sacred divine mission. I am a better candidate than anyone else to reign over the kingdom after my cousin, may God extend his life."

Countess Morphia: "It seems that you have forgotten you are speaking to your wife. I know you all too well, and I'm aware of your notorious stances on clinging to values. Just a few months ago, you banished Joscelin de Courtenay, your right-hand man, and a few years before that, you coerced your father-in-law and seized his wealth."

Count Baldwin of Bourg: "Enough scolding and chiding from you. You have wounded me by reopening files of my former deeds after I had already clarified my rationale for them. Yet, you persist in faulting and reproaching me."

Countess Morphia: "It seems that I have struck a nerve with you, and now I know your frailty. You always flaunt your virtues and ignore your defects. My sole purpose in this act is to amend you and urge you to abandon those bad ways."

Count Baldwin of Bourg: "I hope you busy yourself with amending yourself before appointing yourself as a reformer for me, for I know what is best for me and my county."

As the conversation intensified, Melisande, the twelve-year-old daughter of the Count and Countess, intervened, trying to soften the heated debate with her distinctive smile. She kissed her father's hand, who had a special love for her, and said:

Melisande: "It seems both of you are very engrossed in political discussions, as if you were rival politicians in a council of rule, rather than in our beautiful house filled with love and affection."

Count Baldwin of Bourg: "Indeed, it is a house with you in it, my little one."

Melisande replied politely to her father, trying to draw his attention that she has reached twelve years old.

Melisande: "My dear father, do you know that I have reached the age of twelve today, and I have become a woman."

Count Baldwin of Bourg: "I wish you would never grow up and remain my little girl so I can continue to show you my endless love."

Countess Morphia: "I cannot help but notice that your love seems solely focused on Melisande, as if Alice and Hodierna have no share of it."

Baldwin of Bourg: "I hold great love in my heart for Alice and Hodierna, no less than for Melisande."

Alice: "Father, I must say, you always seem to prefer talking to Melisande and rarely give me much of your time."

Baldwin of Bourg: "My dear Alice, I love you just as much as I love Melisande."

Melisande, replying to Alice: "I don't know why you're jealous of me, as if I'm not your elder sister who loves you very much."

Alice: "Love is not in words but in deeds. Father does seem to favor you over us."

Countess Morphia: "Please, let us not get distracted by this futile argument."

A few days passed, and Roger, the regent of Antioch and son of Richard, proposed to Count Baldwin of Bourg's sister, as part of a plan orchestrated by the Count. The wedding took place in Antioch, with a grand celebration attended by Count Baldwin of Bourg, his family, and their entourage.

Then this dialogue takes place between Count Baldwin of Bourg and his wife, Morphia, after they returned from the wedding ceremony.

Countess Morphia: "I suppose your plan to gain control of the Kingdom of God is underway. You have successfully arranged this political marriage with the Antioch regent. Is your next move to become the ruler of the Crusader state, especially since Norman Countess Adelaide hasn't produced an heir to the Kingdom of Jerusalem? Maybe her husband, King Baldwin of Boulogne, will discard her after he has taken all her wealth from their marriage."

Count Baldwin of Bourg: "Indeed, this is just the first step. There will be more to come, but it requires patience and persistence on our part."

Countess Morphia: "What is the next step, my dear Baldwin?"

Count Baldwin of Bourg: "You'll find out when the time is right, but not a moment sooner."

Countess Morphia: "I must admit I feel hurt that you don't trust me to keep your secrets. I have always been the guardian of your secrets and the caretaker of our daughters. It is evident in the way they've been raised with their good manners."

Count Baldwin of Bourg: "Forgive me, my lady. I trust you completely. You play a crucial role in raising our daughters, who will play a significant part in the future of my grand plan."

Countess Morphia: "You mean marrying them off for political gain if you come to rule the Kingdom of God."

Count Baldwin of Bourg: "I hope you'll let things unfold naturally and focus on our daughters and family. Don't trouble yourself with politics and governance. Those matters aren't a woman's concern."

Countess Morphia: "It seems you want to silence me and keep me from expressing my convictions or offering constructive criticism."

Count Baldwin of Bourg: "I apologize, my dear. I didn't intend to offend you. I ask you to dedicate yourself to more important matters, like raising our daughters, who have a promising future ahead."

In the year 1116 AD, news emerged that King Baldwin of Boulogne had divorced his wife Adelaide, the Norman, after just three years of marriage. He did so after depleting the fortune she had brought with her when they wed, thus crushing the hopes of her son, King Roger II, to rule the Kingdom of Jerusalem.

The following candid conversation takes place between Count Baldwin of Bourg and Countess Morphia.

Countess Morphia: "You seem quite pleased to hear this news. You must be confident now that the Kingdom of God won't slip through your fingers."

Count Baldwin of Bourg: "Indeed, I'm relieved that God has spared the kingdom from the follies of the southern Normans, especially Roger, the impetuous one who wasn't content with ruling southern Italy and Sicily but aspired to extend his dominion over the Kingdom of God in the East as well."

Countess Morphia: "I'm astonished at Adelaide's gullibility, trusting that King Baldwin of Boulogne could divorce his Armenian wife. Did she really think that divorce was a simple matter without the approval of our lord the Pope?"

Count Baldwin of Bourg: "Yes, her son Roger's insatiable greed for power clouded his judgment. He didn't even bother to verify King Baldwin of Boulogne's divorce from his Armenian wife before accepting his mother's marriage proposal."

Countess Morphia: "This world is filled with strange occurrences that boggle the mind. How foolish can some people be? And even stranger still is the fact that the king's Armenian wife, Erda, daughter of Thoros, didn't seek revenge for her husband's foolishness by marrying the Countess of Sicily."

Count Baldwin of Bourg: "What choice did she have? She couldn't seek a divorce, could she?"

Countess Morphia: "I can't say for certain. Perhaps she will find a way to seek retribution that we don't yet understand. Regardless, I pray that our troubles end here and that the King's reckless actions don't exacerbate the Kingdom of God's problems."

Count Baldwin of Bourg: "I pray to God to protect the Kingdom of God from all harm and shield it from the threats of its enemies, especially the Muslims and their allies."

Countess Morphia: "By their allies, are you referring to my people, the Armenians?"

Count Baldwin of Bourg: "I mean the Byzantines and their foolish leader, Alexios Komnenos."

Several weeks later, news reached Count Baldwin of Bourg that King Baldwin of Boulogne's wife, Erda, daughter of Thoros, had left for Constantinople, claiming she was visiting her relatives there and her husband believed her. However, upon arrival, she sought a peculiar form of revenge against her husband for marrying the Countess of Sicily. She engaged in multiple illicit affairs with various men as an act of retaliation, with no intention of returning to her husband. In doing so, she brought disgrace upon King Baldwin of Boulogne in her own way.

This conversation then unfolds between Count Baldwin of Bourg and his wife, Countess Morphia.

Count Baldwin of Bourg: "You're right, my dear. He has gravely wronged her with his actions, but her own disgraceful conduct has brought even more shame upon herself than it did upon the King and the Crusaders."

Countess Morphia: "It is truly regrettable that our honor has been tarnished in this manner, with people gossiping about the foolish actions of our leaders in such a degrading manner. It reflects poorly on both our men and women. I hope such incidents will never recur in the future. Your cousin's lack of regard for women and perhaps his deviant behavior might be at the root of these scandals."

Count Baldwin of Bourg: "Let us not delve too deeply into others' affairs. We have discussed it enough, and there's nothing more to be gained from it."

Countess Morphia: "I thank God that we remain purer and more virtuous than those who have harmed the sacred divine mission."

Count Baldwin of Bourg: "I have decided to visit the King and pay my respects at the Holy Tomb of our Lord."

Countess Morphia: "It seems you aim to mend relations with the King so that he doesn't forget you're a strong candidate for his succession. His old age has taken a toll on him, and it appears his brother and heir, Eustace, has no intention of returning to the East after hastily departing for France following the conquest of the Holy Land twenty years ago."

Count Baldwin of Bourg: "Indeed, the King is in dire need of counsel and support, especially since he has been led astray by the wretched priest Arnulf, who justified his heinous act of marrying the Countess of Sicily."

Countess Morphia: "It seems your commitment to the holy cause has strengthened as your cousin ages. You weren't by his side during the darkest days, such as when he was besieged at Tiberias by the forces of the Muslim campaign led by the governor of Mosul, Mawdud, for over two months five years ago. You didn't come to his aid or lift a finger. If it weren't for reinforcements from Prince Antioch Roger, son of Richard, and Count Tripoli Pons, son of Bertrand, along with Western forces arriving by sea, he might not have been saved. They were the ones who forced the Muslims to lift the siege."

Count Baldwin of Bourg: "You seem quite eager to tally my faults and paint me as a coward who abandoned the holy quest."

Countess Morphia: "Well, it is clear that you're more determined than ever to seize the Kingdom of God."

Count Baldwin of Bourg: "Time will reveal my true intentions in safeguarding the Kingdom of God and assisting the king in its protection."

Countess Morphia: "Yes, time will indeed tell us what you have in mind."

Count Baldwin of Bourg marched with his forces toward the Kingdom of Jerusalem. As he neared the kingdom, he received news of his cousin, the King's death. The King had perished while leading an exploratory campaign in Pelusium, near the border of Fatimid Egypt and his kingdom. He fell to his death after eating a fish meal he caught from the Nile River there. Count Baldwin then made his way to Jerusalem, entering through the eastern gate, while the King's funeral procession entered from the western gate in a rare coincidence. People were occupied with preparing for the King's funeral and bidding him farewell, while Baldwin of Bourg was busy securing his rule over the kingdom after his cousin's death.

In light of these events, a dialogue takes place between Baldwin of Bourg and his cousin, Jocelin de Courtenay, Lord of Tiberias and Galilee, who was a vassal of the deceased King.

Lord Jocelin de Courtenay: "We are deeply saddened by the loss of our loyal King, who sacrificed everything for the divine project."

Count Baldwin of Bourg: "My heart is heavy with grief for our departed King, someone I wished to speak with. Yet, God's will called him to join His chosen ones in the gardens of bliss."

Lord Jocelin de Courtenay: "I will never forget how His Majesty comforted me when you banished me from my fiefs five years ago. He honored me and provided me with vast lands in his kingdom. May God have mercy on his soul."

Count Baldwin of Bourg: "I apologize, my cousin, for my actions and the advisors who influenced my shameful act against you. It caused a rift between us, and I regret it deeply."

Lord Jocelin de Courtenay: "Your regret comes five years too late. It is clear that your apology is driven by self-interest. You're now aspiring to rule the kingdom, knowing that your chances are slim with Count Eustace, the King's rightful heir, and the people and nobles supporting him as the future king of the Holy Land."

Count Baldwin of Bourg: "You know well, my cousin, of my earnest desire for a capable and courageous leader to protect the kingdom. I can't think of a better ally than you to help me persuade the patriarch to anoint me as the King of Jerusalem. I promise to grant you the county of Edessa for you and your descendants in return for your support. I won't dispute it with you, as a token of my gratitude. You have always been my right hand, especially during the darkest days in Edessa and our captivity by the Muslims."

Lord Jocelin de Courtenay: "Your words are kind, but your deeds were anything but. My good deeds were met by nothing but betrayal. Nevertheless, I will align with you, not out of affection, but for my own interests. But I will need your solemn pledge to grant me the county of Edessa for myself and my heirs."

Count Baldwin of Bourg: "I hope you can find it in your heart to forgive your cousin. Our shared blood should strengthen our cooperation for our mutual interests and the interests of God's chosen ones."

Lord Jocelin de Courtenay: "May God have mercy on us if the chosen ones were like you! Anyway, this will serve my own interests, so I will need to bribe Patriarch Fulcher. You know how this old man who drools over money more than anything else? He is also one of those 'chosen ones' you speak of."

Count Baldwin of Bourg: "How loyal you are, my cousin! Satan almost caused enmity and discord between us, but it seems God's will is for us to unite on the path of good."

Lord Jocelin de Courtenay: "God save our souls if your every whim is labeled as God's will! You seem to attribute every desire of yours to divine intention!"

Count Baldwin of Bourg: "I sense the bitterness still lingers in your heart, but I will soon demonstrate my loyalty when I assume the rule of the kingdom. My commitment to you for supporting our common cause will be unwavering."

Lord Jocelin de Courtenay: "Spare me the empty words and meaningless speeches. I know you too well, and I know that it is not God's will guiding you, but your desires and whims. As for God's elect you talk highly of, they are nothing but slaves to their own lusts and remember God only when they're in trouble."

Count Baldwin of Bourg: "Let us end this argument. I expect you to play a crucial role in persuading the leaders, dignitaries, and especially the Patriarch to accept my reign as the king of The Kingdom of God."

Lord Jocelin de Courtenay: "The Patriarch will indeed play a significant role, but convincing most of the noblemen will be challenging. They firmly believe in Count Eustace's right to rule, being the late King's brother. It won't be easy to sway them, for they have principles beyond bribery."

Count Baldwin of Bourg: "I believe that no one can do a better job than you in convincing them. You have a remarkable track record in persuasion, even with our Muslim adversaries. Remember how you convinced the governor of Mosul, Jawali, to exempt us from paying ransom when you offered yourself as a hostage?"

Lord Jocelin de Courtenay: "And what gratitude did I receive for my sacrifice? You rewarded me by stripping away my lands just five years later."

Count Baldwin of Bourg: "Once again, I apologize for my actions. I didn't intend to dredge up the past but to showcase your expertise in dealing with even our Muslim adversaries.

You're the one who orchestrated that remarkable alliance with Jawali in 1108 AD against our enemy Tancred and his Muslim ally, Ridwan, the King of Aleppo."

Lord Jocelin de Courtenay: "I will do my utmost to persuade the leaders and nobles of your rightful claim to rule the kingdom. I hope this time I won't be repaid with unkindness."

Count Baldwin of Bourg: "I swear by God, I won't let you down this time. You'll see my unwavering loyalty in action."

Lord Joscelin de Courtenay wasted no time in winning over Patriarch Fulcher. However, most of the nobles in the kingdom were adamant about sending a swift messenger to France to summon Eustace to claim his brother's throne. Eustace was reluctant to go east, haunted by the horrors he had witnessed in the First Crusade. The images of the dead and wounded still tormented him, even after twenty years since he had left Jerusalem. He had heard a rumor that the Crusaders in the kingdom had pledged their loyalty to Baldwin of Bourg as their new king, so he gave up his right to rule, despite the pleas of the messengers from Jerusalem who urged him to come and annul Baldwin's unlawful oath. Eustace knew he was the rightful heir, being the brother of the late King, but he chose to stay in France. Thus, Baldwin of Bourg secured his legitimacy through Eustace's renunciation, and Joscelin de Courtenay received Edessa as a fief from the new King for his sons. The price of this grant was his recognition of King Baldwin's authority over him as his feudal lord.

With this, King Baldwin of Bourg achieved one of his major goals in ruling the kingdom and bringing Edessa under his feudal control. He also gained more influence over

Antioch by marrying his sister to Roger, son of Richard, the regent of Antioch. He only had to deal with the Count of Tripoli, who did not openly rebel but maintained his independence for another four years until 1122 AD when he refused to pay tribute to the King and showed his clear defiance. King Baldwin II of Bourg gradually realized his ambition of subjugating the Crusader entity under his command, and he had a clear path to dominate all the Crusader lands in the east. However, this also brought him greater responsibilities than he could handle, especially since he was now fifty years old, which was old age in those times.

Then, a new Muslim threat emerged, more formidable than before. In 1119 AD, one year after Baldwin's accession to the kingdom, Ilghazi of Aleppo and Mardin defeated Roger's forces, the regent of Antioch, at the Battle of the Field of Blood with his ally Tughtakin, Prince of Damascus. Roger was killed, along with all his forces, which numbered about seven hundred knights and three thousand footmen. The Crusaders called this battel the Field of Blood because of the severity of their losses. King Baldwin II rushed with his forces to save Antioch, entered the city, arranged its affairs, and entrusted its leaders, especially its Patriarch, with its governance. But whether the Patriarch had ruled it directly or served as a regent for the legitimate young prince who is still in Italy under the protection of his uncle, the actual authority remained in the hands of the King. It is worth mentioning that Antioch's legitimate prince, Bohemond II, was only about twelve years old at that time. King Baldwin then returned to his capital, Jerusalem, bearing the responsibility for both Antioch and his kingdom.

After a long time apart, this dialogue takes place between King Baldwin of Bourg and his wife Morphia.

Morphia: "You have neglected me and our daughters for the sake of the kingdom. You spent nine months in Antioch and didn't even bother to see us. Perhaps you found another woman to keep you company and used the excuse of protecting the Kingdom of God and your great desire to control it as a cover."

King Baldwin of Bourg: "You know how much I love you and our daughters. I would never, for a second, think of dishonoring myself as others have done with disgraceful deeds that damage their reputation and The Kingdom of God."

Morphia: "I hope that the kingdom you inherited doesn't distract you from caring for your family. Remember that they are the most valuable things you have in this world."

King Baldwin of Bourg: "I am well aware of my duties, for I am the most competent to fulfill them and defend all the states of the Kingdom of God, especially Antioch, which lost its prince a few months ago."

Morphia: "Must I remind you that you must be crowned in an official, grand ceremony, with me crowned as the queen?"

King Baldwin of Bourg: "I was already crowned by the kingdom's patriarch a year ago, with everyone's approval."

Morphia: "You should have waited for me to come from Edessa so that we could be crowned together as the King and Queen of the Kingdom of God."

King Baldwin of Bourg: "The kingdom was, as you know, in great danger, and that's why I was crowned quickly; time was not a luxury we had."

Morphia: "Oh, yes, you couldn't bear to wait, as you had to be crowned before the arrival of Count Eustace, the rightful heir to succeed his brother, King Baldwin of Boulogne."

King Baldwin of Bourg: "I told you that everyone agreed on choosing me as the successor to King Baldwin of Boulogne. I was his nearest kin in the east, while his brother Eustace was living far away in France. He chose to go back to his fief in France when he learned that I was unanimously chosen by the religious and secular leaders of the kingdom."

Morphia: "Anyway, I don't care about this futile argument, for I am resolved to be crowned."

King Baldwin of Bourg: "Very well, my lady Queen Morphia, you will be crowned in a week in a splendid celebration befitting your high status, and all the people of the kingdom will witness how the first Queen of the Kingdom of God is crowned."

Morphia: "I thank you, my lord and king, for your loyalty and love for me. You are a good husband and a caring father to your family and our precious daughters."

King Baldwin of Bourg: "All I do is preserve my family and my kingdom for my heirs after me. I pray that you will bear me a son who will inherit."

Morphia: "How I long for that day when I will have a son who will safeguard our rule in the Kingdom of God."

After a few days, Morphia was crowned queen in a grand celebration attended by both nobles and commoners of the kingdom. A few months later, she gave birth to a new daughter, and she showed signs of sadness because she did not have a son to preserve his father's throne. The king went to console her.

King Baldwin of Bourg: "I praise God for your well-being and thank Him for blessing us with this beautiful daughter whom I have named Joveta. She will only deepen the love I have for you and our daughters."

Queen Morphia: "I appreciate your beautiful sentiments, and I thank God for blessing us with this lovely daughter who will fill our house with joy."

King Baldwin of Bourg: "I will do my best to prepare our daughters for their great responsibilities, especially Melisende, who will rule the kingdom after my passing. I will choose a suitable husband for her who can share the responsibility of the kingdom with her until she has a son who can succeed his father as ruler."

Queen Morphia: "It seems you are devising a perfect plan for the future, aiming to secure your hold over the entire crusader entity. There seems to be no command or prohibition except by your will… What a tyrant king you are!"

King Baldwin of Bourg: "And what a tyrant queen you are!"

This dialogue concludes with laughter, a rare experience for them, as their marital life had been marked by excessive seriousness. One might think they were not spouses but rival leaders.

Three years later, in the year 1122 AD, one of the Turk Muslim leaders, Balak ibn Bahram ibn Artuk, captured Count Joscelin de Courtenay, the Count of Edessa, in an ambush. King Baldwin of Bourg rushed to take over Edessa, fearing it would fall into the hands of the Muslims. On his way to Edessa, he also fell into an ambush set by Balak near the castle of Karkar. Balak sent the King to his cousin, Joscelin de Courtenay, in Harput Castle to keep him company and remind him of their first captivity in Mosul between 1104 AD and 1108 AD.

The news of the King's capture struck terror in Queen Morphia's heart. She wanted to assert her authority, being the crowned queen, but the Crusader leaders viewed her with suspicion and ignored her presence. They instead appointed Eustace Grenier as the temporary ruler of the kingdom until the King's release. Queen Morphia begged the leaders to ransom her husband and offered to pay the entire ransom from her own money. However, the leaders deliberately ignored her, not wanting her to appear as the heroic woman taking the initiative to free her husband. Yet, the Crusader leaders failed in their duty toward their lord by arranging his ransom. Realizing the leaders were neglecting her husband's release, the Queen paid a large sum of money to a group of brave men from her Armenian kin to attempt a daring rescue of her husband by force.

Fifty Armenians managed to seize the fortress of Harput through a trick and freed the King and Joscelin de Courtenay from captivity. Joscelin de Courtenay suggested that the King keep the fortress, while he went to the Crusaders to gather a large force to return to the fortress and fight the Muslims. Joscelin de Courtenay went to Antioch, where its patriarch advised him to go to Jerusalem to seek help in supporting the King in Harput. He gathered forces from Jerusalem and Antioch, heading toward Tell Bashir, which belonged to his county. There, he received news that Balak had recaptured the fortress of Harput and captured the King again, sending him to Harran. Joscelin de Courtenay, however, did not set off to Harran to free the King but instead plundered the suburbs of Aleppo. Thus, the Crusaders, including his cousin Joscelin de

Courtenay, forgot their captive King. Queen Morphia remained saddened by her husband's captivity and loss of her position. The leaders did not care about her, forgetting that she has been crowned as their queen only two years ago.

The following dialogue takes place between Queen Morphia and her eldest daughter, Melisende, who was twenty years old at the time.

Melisende: "I can't believe these fools are slacking off in ransoming my father and getting distracted by plundering Muslim lands."

Queen Morphia: "These are the so-called 'God's chosen ones'! Those ungrateful servants betrayed their lord and benefactor. It is as if they're happy about his captivity so they can rule their domains and fiefs without submitting to their King's authority. Can you believe that I had to secretly send those fifty Armenians to free your father? They sacrificed their lives for their King, while these cowards abandoned their captive leader."

Melisende: "If only I had the power and authority over these cowards, I would cut off their hands and tongues for saying what they do not do… What a wretched people they are."

Queen Morphia: "Don't generalize in your judgment, my child. Most of the soldiers and the people are sad and worried about their lord's captivity, but the traitors who hold the affairs of the kingdom, without considering my opinion as their Queen, are the ones who deserve the curse and misery."

Melisende: "When God saves my father from captivity, I will tell him how much they let him down, and I will stir his anger against them. They are nothing but cowardly slackers."

Queen Morphia: "I hope your father returns safely, and we regain our status among the people. The traitors act as if we don't exist, as if the King has died and the kingdom is forever lost to us. May our relief come soon."

Melisende: "We spent four years of our childhood deprived of our father during his first captivity, and today, as daughters of the captive King, we are deprived of his love and forgotten by the subjects of the kingdom."

Queen Morphia: "Fear not, my daughter. Your father will return soon with honor and dignity. He will restore our previous status and take revenge on the traitors."

A few months after the King's capture, Queen Morphia died suddenly after eating some food given to her by one of the kingdom's dignitaries. This plot was likely arranged by those who wanted to eliminate the Queen, who had protested against the lack of attention to her captive husband's release.

On her part, Melisende wasted no time and took action by arranging the poisoning of the temporary governor, Eustace Grenier by poisoning him. He was then replaced by William de Bury, as deputy of the captive King. Thus, twenty-year-old Melisende avenged her mother's murder. It seems that the leaders discovered the secret of the Armenians sent by the Queen to free her husband from captivity and hastened to get rid of her. This is why we do not find any mention of Queen Morphia's death in the accounts of Crusader historians. They also downplayed the death of the temporary governor of Jerusalem.

In 1124 AD, Balak ibn Bahram was killed while besieging the Muslim fortress of Manbij. He was succeeded by his cousin Timurtash ibn Ilghazi, who agreed to release King Baldwin of Bourg in exchange for a ransom of one hundred thousand dinars. Twenty thousand were to be paid in advance, and the rest in exchange for holding the King's youngest daughter, Joveta, as a hostage until the full ransom was paid. The King also promised to return several fortresses to the Muslims, including Al-Atharib, A'zaz, and Kafr Tab, located near the city of Aleppo.

When King Baldwin of Bourg presented his daughter, Joveta, as a hostage to the Muslims, he headed to Antioch before returning to Jerusalem. He spent eight months plundering Aleppo and its surroundings to collect the remaining ransom. He paid the rest of the ransom, and Timurtash returned the child to her father. This suggests that King Baldwin of Bourg was deeply concerned for his daughter's safety and chose to plunder Aleppo to secure the ransom. During this time, he also learned about the death of his wife, Morphia, which greatly saddened him, especially since she had sent people to his rescue from captivity. However, he could not take advantage of the opportunity and fell into captivity again, while Joscelin de Courtenay escaped and saved himself and did not make enough effort to free his King.

In addition, King Baldwin of Bourg discovered that his eldest daughter, Melisende, had arranged the killing of his deputy, Eustace Grenier, during his captivity. He admired her courage and bravery, as she refused to remain silent about her mother's murder and the abandonment of her captive father. However, the deaths of both Queen Morphia and Eustace

Grenier remained a secret known only to those close to the King. This secrecy was maintained to avoid portraying the leaders of the kingdom as traitors who conspired against each other in the public's eyes.

In 1126 AD, the King offered his daughter, Alice, in marriage to Bohemond II, who was still in Apulia, southern Italy, and unable to rule his father's state at that time. The following dialogue takes place between them.

Alice: "I want nothing more than to never disobey you in any matter or desire that is best for us all, but I do not think about marriage right now, my father, for I am still young."

King Baldwin of Bourg: "No, you have become a mature woman, for you are twenty years old. And by this marriage to Prince Bohemond II, you fulfill my desire to preserve our holy entity so that it remains in our hands and no one else's, whether they are Normans from southern Italy or others."

Alice: "Why don't you offer this marriage proposal to my eldest sister Melisende? Maybe she has a desire for Bohemond."

King Baldwin of Bourg: "No, Melisende will inherit me in ruling the kingdom because she is my eldest daughter. And I will choose a suitable husband for her so that they both succeed me in ruling the kingdom. And I hope that she will bless me with a child whom I will crown as king with his parents while I am alive so that I can guarantee that the kingdom will remain in the hands of my offspring."

Alice: "And if I accept this offer, will I stay with Bohemond II forever, or can I stay sometimes with you and my sisters whom I cannot bear to part with? Particularly for Joveta's sake, she lost her mother's tenderness, who was viciously murdered when she was only four years old, then was kept a hostage among the enemies for a year and was about to forget her sisters."

King Baldwin of Bourg: "Bohemond will treat you with decency, and you will find love and tenderness with him. Perhaps you will even forget to visit me."

Alice: "How could I ever forget you, my dear father? You who gave up everything you have, your time, effort, and money for our happiness and the glory of our lord's kingdom?"

King Baldwin of Bourg: "Then I take it you consent to marry Bohemond II."

Alice: "I would never go against your wish, my dear father, for I know that you want what is best for me and my happiness."

The King arranged a political marriage between Alice and Bohemond II. Bohemond II left southern Italy and came to Antioch, as per the King's terms, to stay under King Baldwin of Bourg's authority. Alice and Bohemond II had a splendid wedding ceremony in the city of Antioch, the likes of which had never been seen before. The nobles of the kingdom were in attendance, with King Baldwin of Bourg at their head. Bohemond II was captivated by Alice's beauty and intelligence, seeing in her a faithful wife. He also learned that they shared the wish of freeing Antioch from her father's grip.

Two years later, in 1128 AD, the King approached his eldest daughter, Melisende, with a proposal to marry his kinsman Count Fulk. Fulk was approximately fifty years old, twenty-five years older than Melisende, and still residing in France.

Strangely, Melisende agreed to marry this older man without hesitation. It is worth mentioning that in those days, reaching the age of fifty was uncommon. People usually did not live that long. It seemed that Melisende favored the idea of marrying an older man, perhaps hoping to exert control or anticipating his early demise, allowing her to rule the kingdom, whether or not she had his child. King Baldwin of Bourg organized a grand celebration in Jerusalem for his beloved daughter Melisende's marriage.

In 1127 AD, Alice gave birth to a daughter with Bohemond II, and they named her Constance. Two years later, Melisende had a son, whom his grandfather named Baldwin after himself, hoping to ensure his name's legacy in the ruling of the kingdom.

However, in February 1130 AD, tragedy struck as Bohemond II was killed in a battle with the Muslim prince Ghazi ibn Danishmend, Ruler of Sivas. Antioch's army suffered a significant loss, and King Baldwin of Bourg rushed with his forces to protect the city from falling into Ghazi's hands. Shockingly, Alice ordered her troops to shut the city gates in front of her father and his forces. She even sent a message to the Muslim ruler of Mosul and Aleppo, Atabeg Imad al-Din Zengi, offering to give up Antioch in exchange for his support and to be appointed as his deputy, effectively betraying the Crusader cause.

The King was furious when he discovered that his daughter had defied his authority over the lord's kingdom. However, he managed to enter the city with the assistance of his loyal supporters from Antioch's forces, who honored him because he had ruled the state for eight years before entering into a political marriage deal in 1126 AD with the deceased Prince Bohemond II of Antioch, who married his daughter, Princess Alice.

King Baldwin of Bourg then captured those who had plotted against his authority in the city of Antioch and executed them. He also sternly reprimanded his daughter, showing no leniency as he furiously criticized her for defying his authority. The King's response was harsher toward those his daughter had incited to disobedience than toward his daughter herself, the planner of the disobedience.

In the end, he imposed his conditions on her and had her reside in one of her fiefs, either Latakia or Jabala, which had been given to her by her late husband, Bohemond II, as a dowry before their marriage. He appointed his kinsman, Count Joscelin de Courtenay, as the guardian of the rightful heiress, Princess Constance, the daughter of Bohemond II, who was only four years old at the time. Joscelin would watch over her until she reached an age to marry someone suitable to rule the state alongside her. Then, the King made his way back to Jerusalem.

This dialogue happens between King Baldwin II and his eldest daughter, Melisende, following the recent events.

King Baldwin of Bourg: "How could your sister betray me like this and conspire with our Muslim foes, even going so far as to offer them the land that we fought so hard to defend? She wanted to hand it over to the enemy of our nation, Zengi, who rules with an iron fist in Syria and the Island of Euphrates. He covets the realm of Damascus to add to his domain, which would unite all the Muslim lands of Syria, making it easier for him to wipe us out."

Melisende: "Forgive her not, my gracious father, for your wrath is just at this foolish daughter who forgot that she was nurtured in the arms of her late mother Queen Morphia and Your Majesty, and was fed both the love of God and the Kingdom of God. It is as if someone deceived her and wiped the love of God in her heart away and replaced it with the love of chaos and tyranny over people."

King Baldwin of Bourg: "I have been so grieved that I have been struck with weakness, frailty, and bitter sorrow. With this calamity that befell me, I feel that my end is nearing, for I did not see such treachery coming, especially from Alice, my own flesh and blood."

Melisende: "I am sorry for you, my father, for any harm that has come to you from this witless one. My dear husband, Fulk, and I will not allow her to take over Antioch, after God calls you to his side after a long life. We will not allow her to rob her daughter Constance of her rightful claim to rule the state."

King Baldwin of Bourg: "I will call for a meeting next week for all the nobles of the kingdom and crown you and your husband Fulk as co-rulers of the kingdom, as well as crown my grandson Baldwin III king over the Kingdom of God, which he will safeguard as his grandfather did."

A grand meeting was held, attended by all the nobles of the kingdom led by the Patriarch, Fulk, Melisende, and the child Baldwin, who did not grasp what was happening around him. The three were crowned by the King, who was worn out by illness and showed clear signs of feebleness, as if he was bidding his subjects farewell. While Melisende stood out in this crowd as the mistress of glory and decision-making, her old husband appeared weak, showing signs of a weak personality and lack of resolve. It seemed that things were heading towards a new era, an era of Queen Melisende, rather than an era of King Fulk.

A few days later, King Baldwin II died on August 21st, 1131 AD. The three were crowned again by the hand of the Patriarch of the Church of the Holy Sepulcher. Thus, it was confirmed that the rule would become a partnership between Queen Melisende and King Fulk, until Baldwin the child took over the affairs of the kingdom after his father Fulk's death.

This dialogue takes place between King Fulk and Queen Melisende on the night of their coronation.

King Fulk: "The coronation was a glorious spectacle, and you radiated even brighter with the royal crown atop your head, despite the sorrow in your eyes."

Queen Melisende: "My father's loss shattered my soul and filled my heart with grief. How could it not show in my eyes? He was a kind and generous father who dedicated himself to the kingdom and his family, especially me. He named me after his mother and cherished me more than my sisters, though they sensed it, they never complained to our father."

King Fulk: "My beloved queen, you have won the hearts of all the people. I am honored to have wed you and joined your noble and esteemed family."

Queen Melisende: "We thank God for blessing us with such a distinguished family, revered by the Franks. My father, uncle, relatives, and Lord Hugh, Count of Jaffa, were all outstanding individuals, upon whom my father relied during his wise rule of the kingdom. I will not let their deeds, expertise, and loyalty go to waste as they served the Kingdom of God faithfully."

King Fulk: "They are indeed exceptional individuals whom I also trust, for they are my kin as well as your father's."

Queen Melisende: "I hope our authority over the other Crusader States will continue, just as it did during my father's rule. He had a way of taming their rulers, and we will spare no effort in preserving his legacy."

King Fulk: "I will not falter in this regard and will follow in your father's footsteps to unite the Kingdom of God."

Queen Melisende: "I will do my part in this grand mission, in which my father made you my partner. We will jointly govern the Kingdom of God, and I hope you will be by my side, providing your unwavering support."

King Fulk: "Likewise, I hope for your support in ruling the Kingdom of God, a responsibility bestowed upon us by God, and a great honor."

A new era dawned, marked by conflict and rivalry between Queen Melisende and King Fulk as they vied for power and authority. The first test came when Alice, the princess of Antioch, emerged from isolation and returned to rule the state with her allies. Fulk hesitated to send her back to her domain, as her late father had done, and she grew bolder. She convinced Joscelin de Courtenay, the Count of Edessa, to join her alliance.

Joscelin, more a vassal to Alice than a guardian to her daughter Constance, the rightful heir, seized the opportunity after King Baldwin of Bourg's death and Fulk's ascension to the throne to free himself from allegiance to Jerusalem. He refused to be a vassal to the new King.

Alice went further, winning over Pons de Boutiller, the Count of Tripoli, possibly through bribery or persuasion. It is possible that Pons' wife, Cecilia, Fulk's half-sister, had incited her husband against her brother. Cecilia, the illegitimate daughter of King Philip I of France, had married Pons de Boutiller, following the will of her first husband, Tancred. Pons had taken over the county of Tripoli nineteen years ago, in 1112 AD, after his father's death.

Alice's initial attempt to break free from her father's authority had failed a year ago after her husband Bohemond II's death. However, now she led a strong alliance that sought to end Jerusalem's authority over them permanently. These states' princes and counts refused to accept Fulk's rule, even after his three years in the kingdom without gaining loyal supporters and allies to establish the Kingdom of God's authority, as it was in Baldwin of Bourg's days.

After a year of this disobedience, Fulk decided to assert his authority over the rebellious states. He marched his forces toward Antioch, passing Tripoli on the way. There, he defeated Pons de Boutiller's forces, capturing most of them. He made peace with Pons and forced him to submit. Then, he continued toward Antioch to quell the rebellion.

The city opened its gates with the support of those loyal to Fulk. Alice, the mastermind of the rebellion, fled hastily to her domain in Latakia, fearing Fulk's wrath. Her alliance quickly collapsed. Fulk demonstrated his ability to subdue rebels and foil conspiracies with strength and firmness. He stayed in Antioch for a long time to secure its affairs, appointing Renaud Masoie as the new guardian for Constance, replacing the defiant Joscelin de Courtenay.

Any doubts about Fulk's leadership over the Crusader entities would vanish later when he came to rescue Pons de Boutiller, besieged by Zengi's Muslim forces in Barin Castle. Fulk also achieved victory over Zengi's forces near Qinnasrin, solidifying his competence to lead the Kingdom of God, despite the severity of Alice's rebellion.

The King came back to Jerusalem and this conversation unfolds between him and the Queen.

Queen Melisende: "My dear, You have demonstrated your bravery and dedication to preserving the kingdom's unity with your triumphant campaign against the wicked alliance led by the traitor Joscelin de Courtenay."

King Fulk: "I suspect you might not be aware of the true situation in the kingdom. The leader of this alliance wasn't Joscelin de Courtenay but your sister, Princess Alice. She defied your father two years ago, which makes her rebellion against my authority less surprising. Even my half-sister, Cecilia, incited her husband, Count Pons of Tripoli, to revolt against our sovereignty."

Queen Melisende: "Alice defied her father before, and now she defies my authority. As for your sister, she is no concern of mine."

King Fulk: "May I point out to the fact that you were just saying it was Joscelin de Courtenay who led this alliance of evil? And now you say that Alice rose against your authority, I will not bother correct you, and say it was my authority she stood against, for I am the foremost man in the kingdom."

Queen Melisende: "Yes, and I am the foremost woman in the kingdom, I am the one who elevated you to this great position, from your obscure position in the kingdom of the Franks. After you reached the age of fifty, I graced you by agreeing to marry you and share the rule of my father's kingdom with you. My father crowned you with his own hands, as a favor and generosity from him."

King Fulk: "I didn't seek your hand. Your father proposed our marriage to honor you. I come from a noble family; my father was Count Fulk IV, and my mother was Bertrada, the wife of King Philip the Great of France."

Queen Melisende: "Yes, you do come from a very noble family. Your very honorable and chaste mother, Bertrada, was King Philip's lover. Correct me if I am wrong, but he did not wed her legally because he did not obtain the Pope's approval to divorce his first wife. It was his first wife who bore him Constance, who later married Bohemond I, Prince of Antioch. As for your mother of honor and chastity, she gave birth to an illegitimate daughter, Cecilia. Allow me to remind you, as it seems you may have forgotten, that she was the one who incited her husband, Pons, Count of Tripoli, against you. Do you want me to continue recounting the history and deeds of your noble and honorable family and their descendants?"

King Fulk: "It appears, my dear, that we have delved too deeply into a pointless argument. We are kin, and we possess noble morals. However, we are merely flawed children of Adam, who are weak and succumb to our desires. It is God who pardons His servants and forgives their mistakes. We should not engage in name-calling."

Queen Melisende: "I agree; we shall not delve further into this futile argument. We are both partners in ruling the Kingdom of God, and with our cooperation, we will achieve unity and strengthen the kingdom. Our disagreement will only weaken us and our realm. I pledge to be your support as long as you recognize my status and authority in my father's kingdom. I hope these trivial matters do not disturb our harmony. We should not stoop so low as to insult each other or act arrogantly. We both come from noble families, and we are bound by ties of kinship. I pray that God protects us and our family from disintegration and from falling prey to Satan's temptations, for he seeks to sow discord among us, having already deceived some of our followers, the princes of the crusader states, and lured them into disobeying our authority with their vile conspiracy."

King Fulk: "I fear that my prolonged absence from you in Antioch has weakened the strong emotions that bound us together, which were so prominent in the early years of our marriage. Perhaps our preoccupation with managing the affairs of the kingdom has eroded this love. I was engrossed in military campaigns, and you were dedicated to preserving the capital of the kingdom during my absence. You are indeed a capable queen, having demonstrated high competence by working in collaboration with army leaders and dignitaries to manage the holy city during my time away."

Queen Melisende: "I spared no effort, along with my brothers, who are leaders of the kingdom, during your absence, which was quite challenging for me. My thoughts were consumed with concern for your safety, and I longed for our reunion. Nevertheless, our responsibilities within the Kingdom of God are greater than anything else."

King Fulk: "I hope to succeed in managing the affairs of Antioch and achieving peace in the kingdom while enjoying our closeness. You are the home I missed during my campaigns, which I undertook solely to seek God's blessings."

Queen Melisende: "I trust that nothing will distract us from the deep love we share, a love unshaken by any adversity, as pure and sincere as it is, free from personal interests."

King Fulk: "Indeed, I am blessed with such a love, my dear Queen Melisende. I feel closer to you today than ever before."

Only a few months had passed since that conversation, which began with a harsh rebuke and ended with a reconciliation, when whispers began to circulate in the King's court. There was talk and rumor of an unnatural relationship between the Queen and her father's cousin, Hugh, the Count of Jaffa.

It seemed that this relationship was an extension of a long one that had united them since their childhood in Edessa, and perhaps this relationship had become stronger and deeper because of Fulk's preoccupation with Antioch for several months and his leaving the affairs of the kingdom to Melisende, who relied on her relatives and especially Hugh in managing the capital.

The matter escalated to the point that Walter, the lord of Caesarea and Hugh's stepson, accused Hugh in front of everyone of conspiring against the King's life and disobeying him. But no one dared to accuse Hugh of violating the honor of Queen Melisende openly. It seemed that this severe accusation was not expected to be issued in such a blunt and sudden way by Walter, which necessitated an urgent meeting of the courtiers to confront Hugh with this serious charge.

Hugh denied the accusation. The court decided, according to the customs known at that time, that the accuser Walter should duel with his accused stepfather. Hugh refused, and fled to his fiefdom in Jaffa, thus supporting Walter's accusation. Then, Hugh resorted to the Fatimids in the coastal city of Ascalon, which was the only Muslim city at the time that had not yet fallen into the hands of the Crusaders, and asked them for help. However, mediation efforts with Hugh convinced him to return to the kingdom and to his fiefdom in Jaffa.

It happened that one of the Crusader knights at that time made an attempt to kill Hugh, but failed. The knight was captured and sentenced to death. The King stipulated that this knight's limbs be cut off one by one, with his tongue being the last thing to be cut off. In doing so, the King proved that he was not the instigator of this plot against Hugh. The execution was carried out in that gruesome way, thus exonerating the King from the charge of inciting to kill Hugh.

After Hugh's somewhat recovery from the stab, he left the kingdom and headed to his cousin, Roger, Duke of Apulia, in Italy. But it was not long before he died affected by the stab of that knight.

Upon these events, Queen Melisende saw red, furious at those who accused her, even indirectly, and questioned her honor. What added fuel to the flames was the attempt to kill her cousin, Hugh, and then his death affected by his wound, thus, her rebellion rose making the King fear for himself of her revenge against him, as well as those who incited to kill her cousin, Hugh, especially Rohard. He also feared the revenge of her relatives who were influential people in the kingdom since her father's days.

The mediators made great efforts to eradicate sedition at its roots before it could grow. The King yielded to the Queen's conditions, which compelled him to share in the governance of all kingdom matters with her. From then on, he consulted her on every issue, big or small, thus thwarting the attempts of Queen Melisende's enemies to humiliate her and strip her of her powers in governing the kingdom. She emerged victorious, asserting herself as an equal partner in ruling the kingdom, and anyone who attempted to diminish her authority would meet a miserable fate, even if it were her husband himself.

She asked Fulk to allow her sister Alice to stay in Antioch, and he agreed to this request, despite it conflicting with the wishes of her late father, King Baldwin of Bourg, who had forced Alice to reside in one of his fiefdoms in Latakia or Jableh.

Two months after the fierce storm, a calm dialogue takes place between King Fulk and Queen Melisende.

King Fulk: "My lady, I have been informed that Princess Alice has sent you a private letter for me. Could you please give it to me?"

Queen Melisende: "Certainly, here is the letter. Here you go."

The King takes the letter, breaks the seal, and reads it carefully. He lowers his head, deep in thought. His wife notices his deep pondering and asks if something has happened to her sister.

King Fulk: "No, my lady, she is well. She is also pleased with you and me, especially after we allowed her to stay in

Antioch. The Patriarch now consults her as the guardian of her daughter, Constance, in managing the affairs of the state. However, she complains that she lost her husband after a marriage that did not last more than three years. She is a young woman who needs a husband to provide her with companionship and support, much as you enjoy my tenderness."

The Queen deeply reflects upon hearing these words. She regrets marrying an old man who does not satisfy her desires, which has driven her to seek fulfillment with her cousin, Hugh, from whom she is now lost. This situation has thrown her into a whirlpool of doubts regarding the preservation of her honor and dignity.

Queen Melisende: "Yes, she is a young woman who was deprived of her husband's affection and caress at an early age."

King Fulk: "I will arrange for the marriage with Bishop Ralph, the candidate for the patriarchate of Antioch, and I will carefully select honorable men for her, considering their character and morals. I suggest Lord Raymond de Poitiers, who hails from a noble family and resides in the court of the King of England. He is fit to manage the state and marry Alice, becoming the guardian of her daughter, Constance, the legitimate heir to the rule of the state, who is now nine years old. He will provide her with companionship and support, much like my situation with Your Majesty in the Kingdom of God."

Queen Melisende: "I agree with you, this is a good choice. However, we must obtain Alice's consent as she is the one who should decide this matter, as it determines her future and personal life."

The Queen sent a letter to her sister Alice, inquiring about her opinion regarding her marriage to Raymond de Poitiers. Alice agreed to the proposal and requested Ralph, the candidate for the patriarchate of Antioch, to arrange her marriage and obtain Raymond's consent. Ralph collaborated with King Fulk to organize Raymond de Poitiers' marriage to Constance, the young daughter, instead of her mother Alice. Ralph also pledged that if Henry, Raymond's brother, asserted a claim to Antioch due to his kinship with Bohemond I, the first prince of Antioch, he would persuade Henry to marry Alice. Considering that Alice still possessed her dowry from her late husband Bohemond II, comprising the coastal cities of Latakia and Jableh. In return for these arrangements, Ralph sought the support of the clergy who opposed his appointment as Patriarch of Antioch.

Raymond de Poitiers embarked on a sea voyage through southern Italy, where he encountered the possessions of King Roger II of Sicily. Raymond believed he had a stronger claim to rule Antioch due to his familial ties to Bohemond's family. To avoid detection and potential arrest by Roger II, Raymond de Poitiers refrained from revealing his true identity as he pursued his intention to marry Antioch's heiress.

As preparations for this unusual marriage were underway, **a serene exchange unfolds between Princess Alice and her daughter Constance.**

Curiously and with the innocence of childhood, Constance inquired: "Mother, if you wed Raymond, will he take the place of my first father Bohemond II, who perished defending us?"

Alice: "He is not your true father, my dear, but he will be like a father to you in his role as your mother's husband. He will cherish you as his own daughter, for his love for you stems from his love for me."

Constance: "I will finally have a father to play with, I grew weary of playing with the little ones."

Alice: "And why did you grow weary of playing with the little ones? You are still young and need to fill your days with joy and laughter."

Constance: "I mean that I like to play with the grown-ups."

Alice: "Do not worry too much about this matter. Your uncle Raymond will arrive soon, and you two can play as much as you want. However, he will also devote himself to the administration of the state, which has suffered since your father's death."

Constance: "How I long to see my new father, especially since I heard he was handsome and loves children."

Alice: "I, too, long for his arrival so that he can fulfill your hopes and the hopes of the state by ruling and protecting it as he should."

Constance: "When will my father arrive?"

Alice: "He will arrive soon, perhaps within a few days."

A messenger arrived in late November of 1136 AD, sent by Raymond de Poitiers, announcing his approach to the state. The people of the state eagerly prepared to welcome Raymond, the prince and bridegroom. Alice, the princess and bride, adorned herself with all her jewels to greet the man of her dreams. She wore a wedding gown that she had acquired from Damascus at a considerable cost, crafted from the finest silk in the world at that time.

Constance, her daughter, also prepared to meet her new stepfather, who was expected to fill the void left by her father.

However, a shocking revelation came from Bishop Ralph, delivering news that struck Alice like a thunderbolt. It was revealed that Raymond had no desire to marry her; instead, he sought to wed Constance, who was barely nine years old at the time.

A heated argument unfolds between Princess Alice and Bishop Ralph.

Bishop Ralph: "I understand, my lady, how deeply this news has affected you. Prince Raymond de Poitiers' actions have been a great insult, a betrayal of our trust and kindness."

Princess Alice: "This accusation you make is not the work of Raymond de Poitiers but rather a scheme concocted by you and your vile master, Fulk. You wretched individuals, who clothe yourselves in the robes of religion while practicing treachery and deception. You claim to be 'the chosen ones of the Lord,' but in reality, you are the chosen ones of the devil."

Bishop Ralph: "I apologize, my lady, for the insult inflicted upon you by my lord King Fulk; it was his plan."

Princess Alice: "No, it was your wicked collaboration with him. You deceived me, you scoundrels, and denied me a role in governing my husband's state, even though my sister Melisende, appointed by my father, shares the rule of the kingdom with her husband and son. You have added the final layer to this grand conspiracy. May God curse you all, you chosen ones of the devil."

Bishop Ralph apologized once again, then left with his head bowed, seemingly acknowledging Princess Alice's accusation that their actions were driven solely by self-interest, even if it meant making alliances with the devil.

Alice, enraged, promptly set off for her fiefdom, leaving the state and her daughter in the hands of those she referred to as "the chosen ones of the Lord." They had orchestrated a plot that rivaled the cunning of the devil himself. King Fulk had gone so far as to conspire with the bishop against Alice and her sister, Queen Melisende, dismantling a significant pillar of female leadership in the state of Antioch. All that remained was to undermine Queen Melisende's power. Alice knew her sister wouldn't remain silent and will, for sure, respond to the insult she and her sister had endured at the hands of her husband, the King, who had portrayed himself as a harmless lamb while conspiring with the ruthlessness of a wolf.

The scheme of Fulk and Ralph was completed when Ralph approached the young Constance and taught her the words she needed to say when Raymond de Poitiers proposed to her. The innocent child did not realize that by uttering those words, she had unknowingly become Raymond's wife in place of her mother, who left in anger without explaining her feelings to Constance.

It took Constance several days to understand that Raymond had become her husband, not her stepfather. After Raymond played with her and gave her most of his attention, she eventually comprehended that she was now his wife and had to fulfill his desires in his own way. Thus, a peculiar marriage, unlike any ever heard of before, unfolded in the Crusader East.

When Queen Melisende learned of this plot, she engaged in a heated argument with King Fulk.

Queen Melisende: "You old fool! Have you forgotten that you would never have been crowned king if it weren't for me and my unfortunate choice of you?"

King Fulk: "My lady, I beg your pardon, but what has come over you? How could you believe the false claims of Bishop Ralph? Do you truly think I would order him to arrange such a marriage or dare to command such a vile scheme? Have you forgotten how deeply saddened I was when Alice delivered that letter to me six months ago? Do you see me as a man so vile that I would commit such an act? It is unjust to accuse me of deceiving Alice and her daughter, whom I was entrusted with. Your esteemed father honored me by crowning me alongside Your Majesty and our son, Baldwin, before his passing. Do you truly believe I would marry a child of nine years old to a grown man, especially when that child knows neither the meaning of marriage nor the rights and duties of a wife?"

Queen Melisende: "Such an eloquent speech it is that the swindler Ralph has taught you! How beautiful are your words when you speak of values, and how ugly are your deeds! You speak of values you only know by name, values you do not understand. While you conspire with the devil itself just to achieve your low aims and lay your hands on my father's kingdom."

King Fulk: "I beg your pardon, but this is the Lord's kingdom and not that of any mortal."

Queen Melisende: "Indeed, it is the Lord's kingdom, whose name you offend and sin in, and deceive the faithful, then you pretend that you serve Him. How base and vile are you, O holy ones of the Lord. And soon you will witness the Lord's wrath."

King Fulk: "Spare me, my lady. I did not intend to dishonor your noble father, the King, or deny his grace upon me by granting me the privilege of sharing the throne with you. I pledge not to make any decision without your consent from now on. I swear by God that I fear the Lord's wrath!"

Fulk says as he remembers the death of Eustace Grenier who was the constable of the kingdom when King Baldwin of Bourg was a captive among the Muslims, and the rumors that suggest that the one who poisoned him twelve years ago was Melisende when she was only twenty years old.

Queen Melisende: "It appears you fear my vengeance and the vengeance of my kin. You have always attempted to portray my relatives as traitors to the kingdom, such as my late cousin, Hugh, whom you wronged. You even went so far as to attempt his murder, which led to his demise from that injury. I do not threaten anyone, nor do I seek vengeance, for I was raised in the embrace of a noble and virtuous family that upholds morals and oaths. We are not like beasts who betray the honorable, as you did with my noble sister, Alice."

King Fulk: "I vow to you, my lady, that I will remain loyal in my love for you and your family. I will not tolerate any insults towards them from now on, nor will I pay any heed to slander from those feeble souls who seek to stir up strife between us."

Queen Melisende: "I demand that you send a messenger to Alice in Latakia to offer a sincere apology for your actions, beg her forgiveness, and seek her pardon for the perceived treachery against her."

King Fulk, with all meekness and humility: "I will do so immediately, my lady, and I promise not to incur your anger again. You are the one who gives orders and sets boundaries, and you hold the final say in the Kingdom of God."

Queen Melisende: "Now you understand your rightful place, O majestic king. It has become clear that all the glory and prestige you have achieved would not have been possible without my unfortunate choice of you as a husband and partner in ruling my father's kingdom."

The submissive King left the Queen's council after kissing her hand and displaying signs of humility. The King had become a puppet in the iron Queen's hands, causing the old man to fear death daily.

Shortly thereafter, the Queen busied herself with arranging her sister Hodierna's marriage to Raymond, the son of Pons son of Bertrand son of Raymond IV. At that time, Raymond's father, Count Pons, held the title of Count of Tripoli. The Queen seemed to have orchestrated this political marriage to gain influence over the county. Raymond was the rightful heir to the county in case of his father's death, and the King played a significant role in making this marriage happen.

The wedding ceremony took place in the city of Tripoli in 1136 AD, attended by both the King and Queen.

Six months after the marriage, tragedy struck as Count Pons met his end in a surprise attack by Muslim forces from Damascus, who collaborated with the Maronites. The attack occurred near Tel al-Hajjaj Castle, close to the city of Tripoli itself. In the aftermath, Pons' son, Raymond II, was appointed as his successor. Raymond II sought vengeance against the Maronites, local Christians who adhered to the belief in the singular divine nature of Christ, in contrast to the Catholics who believed in His dual nature, divine and human.

This political marriage provided Queen Melisende with an opportunity to tighten her grip on the county of Tripoli. Raymond II had a weak personality, while his wife Hodierna was strong-willed, similar to her sister the Queen.

Months later, the Muslim leader Zengi, ruler of Aleppo and Mosul, launched a surprise attack on the forces of King Fulk and Count Raymond II of Tripoli near the Castle of Barin. Zengi swiftly defeated them and captured Raymond II. The King retreated with his defeated forces to the Castle of Barin, where Zengi intensified his siege. In exchange for a large ransom of fifty thousand dinars, Zengi agreed to release Raymond II, and the siege was lifted.

Shortly afterward, the forces of Edessa, under the command of Count Joscelin II, and the forces of Antioch, led by Raymond de Poitiers, arrived to rescue the besieged forces. King Fulk, fearing accusations from the queen of negligence in releasing her sister's husband and brother-in-law, had hastily accepted Zengi's offer to secure Raymond II's release.

After a short while, the forces of Edessa, under the command of Count Joscelin II, joined by the forces of Antioch led by Raymond de Poitiers, arrived to rescue the besieged forces. Notably, Joscelin II had succeeded his father two years prior to that battle. In response, King Fulk hastily accepted Zengi's offer to release Raymond II, fearing that the Queen would accuse him of negligence in not securing her sister's husband's release, who was also his brother-in-law.

This dialogue takes place between the Queen and the King after his return from that campaign.

Queen Melisende: "I did not expect you would show such weakness against Zengi's forces. How quickly you fled from the battlefield in terror, as if you were helpless rabbits!"

King Fulk: "Excuse me, my lady, we did not run like rabbits. We faced him fiercely, but it was to no avail. He had the upper hand, since he was superior to us in numbers."

Queen Melisende: "He was only superior to you in courage, daring, and in love of death. And you were superior to him in love of life."

King Fulk: "We beg you, my lady, to believe us when we tell you that war is about deception. Zengi surprised us with a crushing attack, and we were not ready."

Queen Melisende: "I hope such a situation does not repeat itself. Our brother-in-law, Raymond II, fell easily into the hands of our enemies. Anyway, I thank you for paying his ransom. You did not abandon him as the cowards did when my father, the King, was captured thirteen years ago, by leaving my late mother, Queen Morphia, who showed great courage and determination, to deal with saving him from captivity, and sending troops of the honorable Armenians to his rescue."

King Fulk: "I have been burdened with the great responsibility of preserving the safety of all the sons of the kingdom, especially those who are related to Your Majesty, like our brother-in-law, Raymond II."

That period marked a significant development in the relationship between the Crusader state in the East and the Byzantine Empire. The Crusader project could generally be seen as a response to the request for help made by the Byzantine Emperor Alexios Komnenos to Pope Urban II forty years ago in 1093 AD. However, the enormous number of participants in the First Crusade struck fear into the Emperor, as they nearly destroyed his kingdom and occupied his capital. Consequently, he compelled the Crusader leaders to individually swear feudal loyalty oaths. In return, these leaders pledged to surrender any regions they conquered from the Muslims to the Emperor, who would then have discretion over them. He could grant them to one of the leaders who had sworn allegiance to him or assign them to one of his Byzantine followers. The Emperor also promised to provide the Crusaders with material support, including money, weapons, and equipment, as well as moral support in the form of judges and others.

However, as events unfolded, accusations arose. The Crusaders accused the Byzantines of betrayal, claiming that they had failed to provide aid. Simultaneously, the Byzantines accused the Crusaders of breaking their vows by not returning the lands they had seized from the Muslims to Byzantine sovereignty. Antioch, in particular, was a city of great political and religious importance to the Empire.

Tensions reached a breaking point when Crusader King Fulk arranged the marriage of Constance, Princess of Antioch, to Raymond de Poitiers at the end of 1136 AD without seeking permission from the Byzantine Emperor John II Komnenos. This decision infuriated the Emperor, who subsequently decided to take Antioch by force after the Crusaders had refused to hand it over peacefully to the Byzantines forty years ago. In 1137 AD, Emperor John marched with his substantial forces and reclaimed the region of Cilicia for Byzantine sovereignty. This region had long been under the rule of an Armenian prince loyal to Antioch. The Emperor then imposed a siege on Antioch but lifted it when Raymond de Poitiers and Joscelin II, Count of Edessa, pledged to assist him in a joint Byzantine-Crusader campaign against the Muslims in the Levant the following year. The joint campaign aimed to occupy Aleppo and Shaizar, two Muslim cities. If successful, the Emperor agreed to hand over Aleppo and Shaizar to Raymond, while Raymond would relinquish Antioch to the Byzantines if he achieved his goals.

The joint Byzantine-Crusader campaign proceeded as planned, but the expected formidable alliance turned into a fiasco due to deliberate undermining by the Crusaders, resulting in its failure. Nevertheless, the Byzantine Emperor was not prepared to relinquish his claim to Antioch. In 1142 AD, he laid siege to the city once more, and Raymond de Poitiers was on the brink of surrendering it. However, the defiant citizens of Antioch refused to yield, and the Emperor feared the citizens would defeat his forces. Reluctantly, the Emperor agreed to lift the siege under one condition: he would return the following year.

In 1143 AD, the Emperor John returned with his forces to Cilicia, where an unexpected turn of events occurred. While on a solitary hunting trip near Ain Zarba, he suffered a minor hand injury that developed into a deadly infection. Despite medical advice to amputate his hand, he adamantly refused and succumbed to the wound in April 1143 AD. He was succeeded by his younger son Manuel, who had been with him on the campaign. To prevent challenges to the throne, Manuel arrested his older brother Isaac in Constantinople. Thus, the Byzantines failed to subdue the Crusaders of the East during the reigns of Alexios Komnenos and his son John.

However, the new Emperor Manuel pursued a different approach with the Crusader state under the unfolding circumstances of the coming years. In November 1142 AD, King Fulk and his wife, Queen Melisende, went on an excursion near Acre. It was a chance for the couple to escape their dull routine, shed the burdens of governance and administration, and enjoy a new atmosphere of simplicity and pleasure. However, fate had a surprise in store for Fulk during this outing, transporting him to another world—the world of death. While chasing a rabbit with his guard, he fell from his horse and struck his head on the saddle. He lost consciousness due to a fatal injury but had not yet taken his last breath. Melisende rushed to his side, expressing her grief over this great calamity. She tore her clothes, pulled her hair, beat her chest, and lamented like a bereaved mother for her only child. This portrayal of her love for her husband seemed genuine, perhaps forgetting the threats she had made to him only a few months ago if he continued to limit her freedom in ruling the kingdom. The Queen played the role of the grieving widow for a husband she may not have truly loved, as she prepared to welcome a new era, one where she would be freed from the grasp of the old king who had deprived her of the opportunity to control the Kingdom of God.

The new coronation of the queen alongside her son took place on December 24, 1142 AD, in the city of Jerusalem, coinciding with the celebration of Christ's birthday.

This dialogue takes place between Queen Melisende and Constable Manasses, her cousin and right-hand man in ruling the kingdom. The Queen had appointed him as the constable of the kingdom, commanding the knights of the realm.

Constable Manasses: "Your Majesty's presence at your coronation was magnificent. Your face radiated with light and beauty, and dignity enveloped you from head to toe. I witnessed the love in the eyes and smiles of the nobles and leaders, their hope for a new era marked by the strength and unity of our kingdom, and their determination to confront our adversaries, who have troubled us since Atabeg Zengi began his active efforts to unify Syria and Upper Mesopotamia. How I longed to defeat this courageous man, to capture him as a prisoner, and to humiliate him in retaliation for his capture of Raymond II, Your Majesty's brother-in-law, six years ago."

Queen Melisende: "I appreciate your kind words and for acknowledging my beauty, which I believe reflects the heritage of both the Latins and the Armenians. Regarding your concerns about Atabeg Zengi, they are well-founded. He easily overpowered the forces of the late King Fulk, capturing Raymond in February of 1130 AD, twelve years ago. During that time, Zengi nearly obtained Antioch from my impulsive sister Alice, following the death of her husband Bohemond II. It was only thanks to my father's wisdom that Antioch was not lost long ago, and the Kingdom of God was preserved. Today, I aspire for all of us to lead the kingdom towards strength and sovereignty over our adversaries, particularly that haughty Atabeg."

Constable Manasses: "Your Majesty, you will find in me a staunch supporter and your right-hand man. I am also committed to being a good mentor in preparing your son, King Baldwin III, for the responsibility of ruling the kingdom when he comes of age. I will spare no effort in guiding him for this immense task."

Queen Melisende: "Please, do not concern yourself too much with Baldwin's affairs. He is preoccupied with his amusements involving the daughters of the nobles. He frequently moves from one girl to another, indulging in his pleasures. It seems he excels in this pastime. While he tends to his desires, we are tasked with the weighty matters concerning the Kingdom of God."

Constable Manasses: "Your Majesty, you are the best judge when it comes to handling your son's affairs. Your authority is unquestioned, and I am here to serve as a devoted servant to his mistress, who brings glory and honor to the Kingdom of God."

Queen Melisende: "It is evident that you are following the right path to fulfill the needs of the Kingdom of God and its Queen. I have endured much injustice with a husband who robbed me of my youth and insulted what I held dear. He even incited his followers to harm the late Hugh, Count of Jaffa, with whom I shared a close and innocent friendship since our childhood."

Constable Manasses: "You will find me to be a loyal follower to Your Majesty, with a deep understanding of her sensitive feelings, and I aim to provide her with peace of mind and complete comfort, compensating for the years that have passed."

Queen Melisende: "All I need is someone who understands my thoughts, desires, and my love for freedom, which I will not allow to be restricted anymore, or cast me away from the rule of the kingdom as my late husband did over the last twelve years."

Constable Manasses: "Your Majesty, you will find the freedom you seek now that you are the reigning monarch, with all your wisdom."

Queen Melisende: "Thank you for your kindness, Constable Manasses."

Not even a year had passed since Queen Melisende took charge of the kingdom when an appeal arrived from Joscelin II, Count of Edessa, requesting assistance from the Queen. The Atabeg Zengi had laid a fierce siege to his capital, Edessa, while the Count was in Tell Bashir occupied with his desires and amusements.

This dialogue takes place between Queen Melisende and her advisor, Constable Manasses.

Queen Melisende: "It appears our concerns about Zengi were justified. Edessa is now under his relentless siege, and Joscelin II has sent us a desperate plea for help."

Constable Manasses: "Do not despair, Your Majesty, in the face of Zengi's aggression. I suggest we instruct Raymond de Poitiers, Prince of Antioch, to hasten to his aid. Should Raymond fail in this endeavor, we can then issue orders for the remaining commanders of the kingdom's troops to march forth."

Queen Melisende: "Raymond de Poitiers despises Joscelin II more than he despises all the Muslims; they hold deep grudges against each other. How can he risk himself to save him?"

Constable Manasses: "No matter how much enmity exists between them, they will realize that Zengi's threat is a common danger to them and poses a risk to their existence as a whole. A strong message from Your Majesty to your subordinate, Raymond de Poitiers, will compel him to obey your sovereignty."

The Queen sent an urgent message to Raymond, ordering him to hasten and save Edessa from the siege. However,

Raymond did not budge. He gloated at the predicament of his rival, Joscelin II, whose capital was under Zengi's control. As a result, Edessa fell into Zengi's hands. It was the first Crusader capital to fall to the Muslims since the establishment of the Crusader state in the East forty-seven years ago. The Muslims celebrated this great victory and sent delegations to the Abbasid Caliph and Sultan Mas'ud Seljuk with this remarkable news, while the Crusaders mourned this significant loss.

The papacy, grieving at this fall, called for a new Crusade to retake Edessa and preserve what remained of its fortresses, such as Tell Bashir, which Count Joscelin II made the alternative capital for his lost city. The fall of Edessa in December 1144 AD, only a year after Queen Melisende's ascension, marked the beginning of her era with significant setbacks for the Crusader state. It was the first sign of trouble. Consequently, Constable Manasses' wisdom was called into question due to the loss of Edessa. He was expected to rectify this lapse by cooperating with the Prince of Antioch and Count Joscelin II to restore the lost city to Crusader sovereignty. However, speculation suggests that Constable Manasses and Queen Melisende were preoccupied with other matters. Perhaps the beautiful Queen was engrossed in her own affairs rather than preserving the Kingdom of God, which required serious effort and self-sacrifice she might not have been ready to offer.

The responsibility that King Baldwin II once carried was great, and it appeared his eldest daughter squandered it easily. Her father had appointed her and her husband, Fulk, along with their infant son, Baldwin III, as kings just days before his passing. As for King Baldwin III, he was still young and preoccupied with his desires. One might think his mother spared no effort in enabling and indulging him, making him a slave to his bodily desires, with the responsibilities of ruling the Kingdom of God being the least of his priorities. These responsibilities seemed to occupy the Queen and her advisor, Constable Manasses to a greater extent.

It had only been a year since Zengi had liberated Edessa when he launched a large campaign to seize the Muslim city of Damascus and annex it to the kingdom of his lord, King Alp Arslan. It is worth noting that Zengi was the de facto ruler of this kingdom, governing it as the Atabeg (i.e., mentor and guardian) of that king. He declared a Jihad against the Crusaders but learned of a revolt against him in Edessa when he reached the city of Baalbek. He had to change his course, heading to Edessa to subdue the rebels. This forced him to postpone his plan to annex Damascus to the following year. However, fate had other plans, for on the fourteenth of September in 1146 AD, he was killed while besieging the Castle of Ja'bar. His two elder sons divided his kingdom, with Saif al-Din Ghazi ruling Mosul and its domains, while Nur al-Din Mahmud governed Aleppo and its domains on behalf of his brother Saif al-Din Ghazi.

A month had passed after Zengi's death when Joscelin II struck an alliance with the Armenians inside Edessa, took over the city, and massacred the small Muslim garrison.

When the news of Edessa's return to Crusader sovereignty reached the Kingdom of Jerusalem, a dialogue ensued between Queen Melisende, her son King Baldwin III, and Constable Manasses.

King Baldwin III: "I see this as a golden opportunity for us to swiftly send support to Joscelin II and help him stabilize his county, especially given his contentious relationship with his neighbor, Raymond de Poitiers, Prince of Antioch."

Constable Manasses: "My lord, there's no need to dispatch a supporting force, as the threat of our enemy Zengi ended with his demise and the subsequent disintegration of his kingdom."

Queen Melisende: "I envision a peaceful future after Zengi's death, the longtime adversary of the Kingdom of God. I presume his sons will not possess the same strength and courage as he did."

King Baldwin III: "Perhaps Nur al-Din, who has taken control of Aleppo, may pose a more dangerous and formidable threat to our kingdom than his father did. We must address this situation seriously. We cannot afford to be as lenient as we were with Zengi, considering the troubles he caused. He easily captured Raymond II, Count of Tripoli, seven years ago, compelling my father, may God have mercy on him, King Fulk, to pay a substantial ransom for his release. Then, just a year ago, he snatched Edessa from our grasp while we offered feeble justifications for our loss."

Constable Manasses: "Do not fear, Your Majesty, for we are in a much better situation than before, and time will prove my words."

Queen Melisende: "Yes, my son, do not be pessimistic. No one cares about the fate of the Kingdom of God more than we do, as this divine responsibility has been bestowed upon us by God."

King Baldwin III: "I hope my pessimism is unfounded, and that the days to come will bring tranquility and serenity."

Only five days had passed since that conversation when the news arrived, confirming the young King Baldwin III's concerns and exceeding the expectations of the elders, such as Constable Manasses, who was guiding the kingdom toward a gloomy end. Nur al-Din, Prince of Aleppo, acted swiftly and recaptured Edessa, leaving Joscelin II and his Crusader comrades with no option but to flee before the Muslims regained control. Meanwhile, his Armenian allies paid a heavy price for their treachery toward the Muslims and collusion with the Crusaders. Nur al-Din executed the conspirators among them as a warning to deter any future rebellions against his authority. This event served as the first stern warning to the Crusaders, and it spoke louder than words.

This discussion takes place between King Baldwin III, his mother, and Constable Manasses.

King Baldwin III: "My worst fears have come true, and Edessa has slipped from our grasp once again due to our complacency. Western nobles are mobilizing their armies to come to our aid and recapture Edessa, while we failed to provide swift assistance to the Count of Edessa and his comrades."

Constable Manasses: "Indeed, my lord, you saw this clearly, and we were overly optimistic."

Queen Melisende: "It seems that my son possesses keener foresight than we do, heralding a path of leadership and success."

King Baldwin III: "Forgive me, mother, I am no better than Your Majesty, but my deep concern for the Kingdom of God compelled me to worry about its fate. I pray that we never repeat such grave mistakes as this one, which cost us a significant opportunity."

Queen Melisende: "Fear not, my son, with your wise guidance and the support of Lord Constable Manasses and his wisdom, we will safeguard and restore the Kingdom of God under your rule. There's no need for us to fret."

King Baldwin III: "It appears that we are venturing into uncharted territory, as the Muslims are rallying their forces, and we are heading toward fragmentation and discord."

In May of 1147 AD, less than a year after squandering the opportunity to retain Edessa, a Muslim messenger from Busra, named Altuntash, arrived in Jerusalem. Altuntash served as the governor of the strongholds of Busra and Saruj on behalf of the Prince of Damascus, Mujir al-Din Abaq. However, his relationship with the actual ruler of Damascus, the Atabeg Mu'in al-Din Unur, had recently soured.

Altuntash met King Baldwin III, his mother Queen Melisende, and Constable Manasses, and this conversation takes place between them.

Altuntash: "It is a great privilege to visit Her Majesty Queen Melisende and His Majesty King Baldwin III, the grandson of the glorious King Baldwin II, the defender and unifier of the Kingdom of God."

King Baldwin III: "I appreciate your compliment of my grandfather, who devoted himself to the Kingdom of God and its people."

Queen Melisende: "Indeed, my father taught me well, and I, in turn, have taught my son Baldwin well. He has turned out to be faithful and obedient to his mother, nurtured with noble virtues."

Constable Manasses: "The achievements of the glorious King Baldwin II speak for themselves. He excelled in everything, including his choice of King Fulk as the father of His Majesty King Baldwin III, whose Raynaldwn reached the heavens."

Queen Melisende: "Anyway, please, our friend Altuntash, reveal the purpose of your visit."

Altuntash: "I come with a proposal that I believe you will find appealing. I intend to hand over my fortresses of Busra and Saruj, which belong to my oppressive master, Mu'in al-Din Unur, the Atabeg of the Prince of Damascus. In return, you will compensate me with money or a fief far from the State of Damascus to keep me safe from the vengeance of Atabeg Unur, in case you take control of the fortresses."

King Baldwin III: "If you are so afraid of your lord and unable to confront him, why don't you consider abandoning the fortresses and handing them over to him instead of involving us in a conflict with a faithful ally and a friend of ours? Unur entered into a treaty of peace and cooperation with my father, King Fulk, to address our common challenges, especially those posed by Nur al-Din, Prince of Aleppo. Nur al-Din's eagerness to annex the state of Damascus to his realm and unite Syria is well-known, particularly since his elder brother Ghazi passed away some time ago, and his younger brother Mawdud assumed control in Mosul. With this increased freedom, he aims to annex Mosul to the extensive state he aspires to establish. If he succeeds, he will pose a significant threat to our presence in the East."

Constable Manasses: "Nur al-Din's arrogance should not concern you greatly, for we possess enough strength to confront him and thwart his ambitions."

King Baldwin III: "You have often argued that Zengi's threat wasn't to be taken seriously, yet he captured Edessa, and none of us managed to retake it. Even after Joscelin II, the Count of Edessa, liberated it following Zengi's death, our forces didn't cooperate. Choosing to seize two weak fortresses now, within the territory of our Muslim allies and the rulers of Damascus, risks jeopardizing our strategic alliance with them. Nur al-Din might find himself pressured to annex the vulnerable state of Damascus to his authority in response to what he perceives as a threat. It appears that my grandfather Baldwin II's kingdom is on the decline."

Queen Melisende: "Be reassured, my beloved son, for the Kingdom of God is secure and well-preserved, especially under the care of loyal and brave individuals like Lord Constable Manasses and yourself. You both protect and defend against the schemes of our enemies. Furthermore, you should keep in mind that our friend Altuntash's proposal is not mandatory; however, I discern sincerity in his intentions to form an alliance with us."

Constable Manasses: "I am certain that Her Majesty Queen Melisende prioritizes the safety and interests of the kingdom. If we were to agree to annex Busra and Saruj to the kingdom, it would pave the way for us to potentially annex the entire state of Damascus, including the ancient and resource-rich city of Damascus itself. This expansion would enhance our kingdom's prestige and establish our sovereignty over the remaining Latin states in the East."

King Baldwin III: "Are you suggesting that the rulers of France and Germany, as they journey to the East, will not liberate Edessa for its rightful owner, Joscelin II, but rather aim to annex the Muslim state of Damascus to our kingdom? This would grant us the opportunity to extend our kingdom's sovereignty throughout the East?"

Queen Melisende: "Yes, this campaign would serve the interests of the Kingdom of God, and you would become the ruler of a vast kingdom with influence extending across the entire East."

King Baldwin III: "It seems that you are solely focused on advancing your own interests at the expense of other Crusader state rulers, potentially causing them to lose loyalty and submit to our kingdom, which my grandfather, Baldwin II, painstakingly achieved. If the rulers of France and Germany prioritize their interests in the same way you are advocating, and they decide to establish a new Crusader kingdom on the remnants of the Damascus state, it may become a significant rival to our kingdom, potentially monopolizing the zeal of the entire Crusader entity."

Constable Manasses: "I will spare no effort in persuading the Western kings to act in the best interests of the Kingdom of Jerusalem, under your majesties' rule. I have dispatched individuals who are most suited for this mission. The French King Louis VII is married to Queen Eleanor, who is the niece of Prince Raymond de Poitiers, the ruler of Antioch. Perhaps this familial connection will aid Raymond in convincing the French King to support his efforts to annex the Muslim city of Aleppo to his state. However, I will exert my utmost to dissuade the King from forming an alliance with our rival, Raymond de Poitiers, who aims to exploit the forthcoming crusade for his personal gain."

King Baldwin III: "This implies that King Louis VII may be more inclined to please his wife and fulfill the ambitions of her uncle, Raymond de Poitiers, the prince of Antioch, potentially at our expense. It appears that your suggestions, Constable Manasses, may not align with reality. You seem to believe that you can easily influence and guide the European lords toward your objectives. Do you not recognize the shrewdness of these individuals?"

Queen Melisende: "Yes, I have received reports confirming that Louis VII has a deep affection for his wife and is unlikely to deny her requests. Some may even speculate that Queen Eleanor wields significant influence in the Frankish kingdom, possibly overshadowing Louis VII. She possesses a strong personality, akin to mine. His Majesty King Fulk was a loving and obedient husband, meaning he valued my counsel in many matters concerning the kingdom, particularly in the later years of his benevolent reign. May God have mercy on him; he was a devoted spouse. How I wish Eleanor could persuade her husband, Louis VII, to join us in the endeavor to annex Damascus to our kingdom, rather than siding with her uncle, the prince of Antioch."

Constable Manasses: "I hope that we can arrive at a clear decision regarding our friend Altuntash's offer, as he has been patiently awaiting our discussion. Let us keep in mind that he does not speak our language. I hope His Majesty agrees to this proposal. Furthermore, I suggest that Your Majesty personally lead this campaign, as you are well-suited for this significant task, especially since you have reached the age of seventeen. This offers you an opportunity to gain valuable military experience before the forthcoming crusade arrives in the East."

Queen Melisende: "Sir Manasses, your proposal to entrust my beloved son with the leadership of this campaign is a great honor and privilege. However, I worry about the potential risks he may face during this undertaking."

King Baldwin III: "I do not fear death, and I am fully capable of leading this campaign. I agree to Altuntash's proposal, even though I am not entirely convinced of the significance of his forts located in such a desolate area. I will also promptly inform our friend, Sir Unur, the Atabeg of Damascus, about this campaign. We must honor the treaty my father, King Fulk, signed with him, which requires us to notify him before our troops enter his lands."

Altuntash: "Your Majesty, I am grateful for your acceptance of my request, and I hope to repay you for this favor in the near future."

The Crusader army was prepared to march in response to Altuntash's call, who offered his two forts to King Baldwin III. However, before proceeding, the King had to seek permission from Unur, the Atabeg of Damascus, as his army needed to cross Unur's lands. Deliberately, Atabeg Unur delayed his response for a month while seeking assistance from his Muslim allies, particularly his son-in-law, Nur al-Din, the prince of Aleppo, in an effort to thwart the Crusaders' attempt to annex these two forts.

Unur's reply eventually reached his ally, King Baldwin III, taking on a political tone. In his response, Unur reproached the King for breaking his oaths and for accepting the offer made by one of his followers, Altuntash. Altuntash had betrayed his lord, the prince of Damascus, by offering to surrender his two entrusted forts to the King of Jerusalem. Unur reminded King Baldwin III that this act was a clear violation of the peace agreement previously signed between him and King Fulk, who had since passed away.

In response, King Baldwin III sent a letter to Unur explaining his reasons for accepting Altuntash's offer. Unur then dispatched a messenger proposing that Altuntash return under his lord's authority, the prince of Damascus, and hand over his two forts, Bosra and Salkhad, in exchange for compensation with another fief.

Unur subsequently sent another letter to King Baldwin III, offering to withdraw from the campaign and provide financial compensation for the expenses incurred in its preparation. He sought to restore good relations between them and emphasized his sincere commitment to their covenant. Unur also expressed his willingness to address Altuntash's situation peacefully, without resorting to military force.

This last offer from Unur reached the Crusaders through the King's envoy, Bernard Foucher, who was related to the King by kinship. Bernard advocated for a peaceful resolution to the issue. However, some opposed this approach, accusing him of betraying the Kingdom of God's trust and squandering a valuable opportunity by not annexing the two forts, especially Bosra, often referred to as the "Great City." In the end, the impulsive sentiments of the masses prevailed over the wisdom of the wise, and the King was compelled to march with his troops towards Bosra, though the full extent of the campaign's danger became clear only after it had commenced.

This ill-fated campaign to annex Bosra and Salkhad lasted for two weeks, during which the Crusader army endured great hardships and difficulties, nearly perishing entirely.

Following this terrible failure, a dialogue unfolds between the King and his mother.

King Baldwin III: "Bosra was a conspiracy hatched by our enemies to deliver us a fatal blow, and these enemies were not from outside; they were within our midst. Altuntash is nothing more than an agent sent by our adversaries to divert us from our grand objectives. I perceived signs of a plot against us at every turn during this wretched campaign. I wish I could identify the mastermind behind the agent Altuntash, the one who enticed me into leading this disastrous expedition, waiting for my downfall, all the while planning to seize control of the kingdom with the conspirators."

Queen Melisende: "You seem to be insinuating that Constable Manasses is behind this scheme. This is exactly what the enemies of the kingdom want you to believe. They aim to sow discord among us so they can seize power."

King Baldwin III: "I am not a mere puppet in anyone's hands. I witnessed horrors in our campaign, orchestrated by Nur al-Din's alliance with Aleppo and Damascus. They besieged us and encircled our troops for over a week. We were on the brink of annihilation if not for God's mercy, which saved us from them. You once argued that Nur al-Din posed no serious threat. Today, I have come to realize that he is even more perilous than his father. What struck me as most peculiar in this dire campaign was that many of the leaders urged me to escape on my swift horse, leaving them all behind to die as martyrs for the Kingdom of God! It is as if these rascals cared about my safety, when in reality, they sought to eliminate me. I thank God I did not heed their advice, which could have spelled my doom."

Queen Melisende: "My son, you should not make such baseless accusations. The army leaders who offered you that advice are the same leaders who served your father, King Fulk, and your grandfather, King Baldwin II, may God have mercy on their souls. They genuinely care about your safety and the well-being of the kingdom. And Sir Constable Manasses was one of your father Fulk's closest confidants."

King Baldwin III: "Yes, he was close to my father, and to you! It often seems like you value his counsel more than the welfare of the kingdom itself!"

Queen Melisende: "Sir Constable Manasses is a capable leader and one of the most competent among our commanders. I meet with him frequently because I seek his advice on crucial matters of the kingdom. I hope you won't overstep your boundaries with these baseless accusations against Sir Constable Manasses."

King Baldwin III: "I apologize, mother, for speaking without sufficient evidence. My words were driven by a heavy heart after this disastrous campaign."

King Baldwin III repeated his apology to his mother, kissed her hand, and expressed his genuine remorse and humble submission.

After about four months following the disaster at Bosra, news of the second Crusader campaign's advance to the east arrived. Emperor Conrad, the German Emperor, marched at the head of seventy thousand knights, while King Louis VII of France also led seventy thousand knights. The German army reached the East about a month before the French army. After a brief stay as a guest of his brother-in-law, Emperor Manuel of Byzantium, in the capital of the Byzantine Empire, Conrad crossed by Byzantine ships to the Asian side of the continent. He recklessly ventured into Anatolia, which was controlled by the Seljuks of Rum, and in November of 1147 AD, he was caught off guard by a Muslim army led by King Mas'ud bin Qilij Arslan. They launched a thunderous attack near Dorylaeum, resulting in a catastrophic loss for the German forces. Nine-tenths of them were either captured or killed in that disaster, while the remaining survivors fled, including the Emperor himself who barely escaped certain death.

The survivors of the defeated German forces later joined the French army, which arrived a month later under King Louis VII. The Germans shared the news of the calamity that had befallen them a month earlier with their French allies. Nevertheless, the French army remained undeterred and was determined to avenge the defeat that had struck their German comrades.

Emperor Conrad returned to Constantinople with what remained of his forces from Ephesus. During his journey back, he encountered King Louis VII in Bithynia, where they agreed to jointly lead the Crusader campaign despite the loss of most of the German army. However, a majority of the Germans refused to obey their Emperor and chose to return to their homelands through Constantinople. Many of them had lost their wealth and were traumatized by the horrors they had witnessed. It is possible that the French's arrogance in their dealings with the Germans contributed to the lack of cooperation from the German contingent at that stage of the Crusader campaign. Consequently, the idea of a French-German alliance crumbled.

The Crusader historian William of Tyre described the defeat of the German army as follows: "It pleased God's just will that the courage which had distinguished these great princes suddenly collapsed, despite their great numbers. This abrupt downfall occurred after minor skirmishes, leaving behind only a faint trace of their former glory. Their once-numerous army, which had almost seventy thousand knights along with countless infantrymen, saw only one survivor out of every ten. Some died of thirst, others perished by the sword, and still others became prisoners of the enemy. The emperor, along with a few nobles, managed to survive."

In December 1147 AD, only two months after the disaster of the German army, another, albeit less severe, catastrophe befell the French army. While the front of the army was marching separately from the rear, as they were ascending Mount Cadmus near Laodicea, a fierce defeat struck the rear. The King himself miraculously escaped with only a few of his soldiers under the cover of night. The front was unaware of the events that had transpired in the rear until it was too late. The French repeated the same mistakes as their German counterparts. The Muslim army, led by King Mas'ud himself, achieved two swift victories over the two largest Western armies participating in the Crusades for the first time, led by the greatest rulers of that era. Historical sources do not specify the extent of the French defeat and losses, but they were substantial.

The Crusader historian William of Tyre described the French defeat as follows: "On this day, the Franks' splendid reputation was lost in a calamity unlike any other; it was one of the most devastating disasters to befall the Crusaders. This is because their bravery, which had been legendary among the peoples, crumbled and became a subject of mockery in the eyes of their adversaries, after once instilling terror in their hearts."

After news of these disasters reached the Kingdom of Jerusalem, a dialogue takes place between King Baldwin III and his mother, Queen Melisende.

King Baldwin III: "My intuition was indeed correct. Disasters and calamities have befallen the two greatest armies in the West. The German and French rulers spent four years preparing their armies with everything needed to achieve great victories over the Muslims of the East. But, lo and behold, they fell like hailstones at the first strike from a small Muslim force. I could not have imagined that the knights of the West were so cowardly, chaotic, and undisciplined. Both armies committed the same fatal errors—lack of cohesion and separation of their front from their rear. This made it impossible for them to know if disaster had struck one of them, whether it was the front or the rear. How foolish are these kings who do not understand the basics of warfare. The attacks we endured months ago when we marched with the kingdom's army to Bosra were far more numerous than what these kings faced. Yet, we were able to maintain our army's cohesion despite being besieged by forces larger than ours from Damascus and Aleppo throughout the ten-day journey. I succeeded in maintaining my forces' cohesion and safely returning to the kingdom after we were betrayed and Bosra was handed over to Damascus' forces under Atabeg Unur."

Queen Melisende: "Yes, my son, these are disasters that we did not expect to happen to our brethren in Anatolia at the hands of our enemies. I also did not anticipate these disasters to befall the two greatest Western armies led by Emperor Conrad of Germany and King Louis VII of France. Despite the severity of these disasters, I have learned that both rulers are determined to complete their pilgrimage, visit the Holy City, and continue their military campaign with what remains of their forces in alliance with our kingdom's forces."

King Baldwin III: "What remains of their forces is one-sixth of the original number that arrived in the East before the two severe disasters. If they were sincere in their pilgrimage, they could still achieve victory for the Kingdom of God. This requires their support, which we have been awaiting for the past four years. However, I fear that the other Crusader states under our rule might not cooperate with them. I have learned that Raymond de Poitiers, Prince of Antioch, Raymond II, Count of Tripoli, and Joscelin II, Count of what remains of Edessa, each seeks to direct the campaign for his own benefit. Raymond de Poitiers wants to annex Aleppo and Shaizar to expand his state, while Joscelin II aims to reclaim his capital, Edessa, which was lost to the Muslims—a legitimate claim. As for the Count of Tripoli, Raymond II, he is concerned about the arrival of his uncle Alfonso, the Count of Toulouse, who is the eldest son of Count Raymond IV de Saint-Gilles. Alfonso's potential arrival with this campaign could lead to demands for rulership over Tripoli, possibly displacing

Raymond II from power. This is his greatest concern at the moment."

Queen Melisende: "We will dispatch envoys as soon as possible, accompanied by Patriarch Fulcher, to meet with King Louis VII of France in the city of Antioch. Our aim is to persuade him to join our mission of annexing Damascus to our kingdom before Raymond de Poitiers has the chance to convince Queen Eleanor, his niece, to influence her husband, the King, to support his ambition of annexing the city of Aleppo to his state instead."

King Baldwin III: "I have received reports confirming that the relationship between the French King and the Prince of Antioch has deteriorated due to suspicions of an inappropriate relationship between Raymond de Poitiers and his niece, Queen Eleanor. Such rumors may lead to sinful acts that polite conversation dare not mention. How could these individuals dare to violate the honor of their own kin?"

Queen Melisende: "Well said, my son. This scandalous act is a stain on good morals. However, we could view it as an opportunity. We might take advantage of the strain in the relationship between the French King and Raymond de Poitiers. This way, we can win over the French King to our side and achieve the goals of God's Kingdom by annexing the state of Damascus to ours."

King Baldwin III: "The one who said, "One man's misfortune is another man's gain," was right. Even the most dishonorable scandals are welcomed with open arms when they serve our interests."

Queen Melisende: "These are the interests of God's Kingdom, of which you are the leader and lord."

Baldwin III: "Adding Damascus to our kingdom is neither my aspiration nor do I believe it helps achieve my goal or the goal of God's Kingdom. These are the aspirations of Constable Manasses, who is leading God's Kingdom to ruin. His only concern is to achieve his own interests and dominate the rule of the kingdom as he pleases. Even his followers advised me to ride my horse and flee alone when we marched to take Bosra months ago, so that they could get rid of me. Today, Constable Manasses aims to achieve his own goals at the expense of the other Crusader states, whose loyalty he has cost us. We still have no confirmation whether they will participate in the upcoming Crusader campaign or not. The misfortunes that this campaign started with will pale in comparison to the greater tragedies I foresee it ending with."

Queen Melisende: "You are always pessimistic, my son. How could you doubt Constable Manasses's sincere devotion to the kingdom? He has sacrificed everything precious and dear to preserve it and pursue its interests. He is a cunning politician and will succeed in convincing the German and French rulers of the idea of annexing Damascus to us, thwarting the attempts of our rivals, especially Raymond de Poitiers, despite his kinship with Queen Eleanor, the audacious one."

King Baldwin III: "It seems that you are taking pleasure in Queen Eleanor's situation, as if she were the sole blemish on the purity of the Kingdom of God."

Queen Melisende: "I agree, the Kingdom of God is indeed tainted, having a king like you who spends his nights and days amusing himself with women of the kingdom, making them compete to please him."

Baldwin III: "I am sorry, mother, for I did not mean to offend anyone in the Kingdom of God. How could I doubt its purity with you and Constable Manasses gracing it with your virtue?"

Queen Melisende: "You have crossed your limits; I think you need some lessons that remind you of the meaning of purity and virtue."

King Baldwin III: "Forgive me, mother, I made a mistake by making baseless accusations, one that I will not repeat. We are all but human, frail, and fallible. I pray to God to bless the virtuous and keep the wicked at bay."

Queen Melisende: "My son, we are all sinners in need of grace. We have the power to choose between good and evil, but we often stray from the right path. We must cleanse our hearts from covetousness and display our piety before God and men."

King Baldwin III: "I beg God's mercy for my folly and your pardon, mother, for my disrespect."

King Baldwin III bends down and presses his lips to his mother's hand, then departs, silent and humbled.

The German Emperor Conrad spent the winter of 1147 AD in Constantinople before setting sail for the port of Acre, from where he embarked on a pilgrimage to Jerusalem. He received a warm welcome from King Baldwin III, Patriarch Fulcher, and the people of Jerusalem.

Alfonso, the Count of Toulouse, also arrived in Acre, intending to make the journey to the holy city as a pilgrim. Tragically, he passed away suddenly due to illness near Caesarea before reaching their destination. Alfonso had held high hopes for this campaign, but suspicions arose that Raymond II, the Count of Tripoli, had ulterior motives for his uncle. There were speculations that Raymond II might have poisoned him out of fear that his uncle would challenge his rule over the county, sparking conflicts among the Crusader leaders.

Meanwhile, the French King Louis VII, incensed by the dishonorable actions of his wife, Eleanor and her uncle, Raymond de Poitiers, departed from Antioch. He made his way to Tripoli, where he was met by Patriarch Fulcher, who extended an invitation for him to visit Jerusalem. The Patriarch was concerned that King Louis VII might align himself with his relative Raymond II, potentially at the expense of Jerusalem's interests. Upon hearing of the discord between the French King and the Prince of Antioch, Fulcher saw an opportunity to capitalize on it for the benefit of his mistress, Queen Melisende, who sought to redirect the campaign toward her own objectives.

In May of 1148 AD, a conference was scheduled to take place in Acre between Emperor Conrad and King Louis VII, along with the eastern Crusader leaders. Strangely, the leaders convened this conference to determine the next destination for the crusade, seemingly forgetting its original purpose – a response to the Muslim capture of Edessa. Even more peculiar was the absence of three Eastern Crusader princes: Raymond de Poitiers, Raymond II, and Joscelin II, who boycotted this crucial meeting. Only the leaders of Jerusalem attended, led by Queen Melisende and her son King Baldwin III, alongside other prominent figures such as Constable Manasses, Philip of Nablus, Gerard of Sidon, and Patriarch Fulcher. In addition, Robert, the Hospitallers' master, and Raymond, the Templars' master, participated. These military orders had been gaining strength due to their strict discipline and zeal, often tasked with guarding the Crusader fortresses due to the shortage of military forces among the Crusader leaders.

With the absence of the Crusader princes primarily concerned with the campaign, it became evident that Conrad and Louis VII would fulfill Queen Melisende's desire to capture Damascus. However, they did not disclose who would govern the city after its capture. Consequently, when Queen Melisende later discovered their intention to hand it over to Count Flanders, who had recently arrived with the French army, she decided to undermine the campaign to prevent this new Crusader state from challenging Jerusalem's dominance in the eastern Crusader territories.

The Crusaders initiated a relentless siege of Damascus from the west, which lasted for four days. They encountered fierce resistance from the city's defenders, yet they managed to gain control of this well-watered and fruitful region. The city nearly fell into their hands, despite Nur al-Din's vigorous efforts to launch devastating attacks aimed at weakening the Crusader armies besieging the city.

The Crusaders had the city at their mercy, but the cunning leaders of Jerusalem managed to persuade the western rulers to shift the siege from the west to the east, arguing that the eastern side was weaker. The rulers fell for this deception and abandoned the west for the east, only to discover that the eastern side was better fortified and lacked water and provisions. They tried to rectify their mistake, but their scouts reported that the defenders of Damascus had reinforced the western side with wood and stone barriers to impede the Crusader knights. The French and Germans grew suspicious of a plot by the Eastern Crusader leaders to undermine the siege, and in response, they decided to lift the siege on Damascus without consulting with the leaders of Jerusalem.

In a span of no more than five days, the same duration it took to besiege Damascus, the campaign that had been four years in the making ended in a resounding failure, marking the swift conclusion of the Second Crusade. It became evident that Queen Melisende and Constable Manasses had sabotaged the campaign upon learning that the western rulers intended to grant Damascus to Count Flanders. They preferred to see Damascus remain in Muslim hands rather than under Count Flanders, who would establish a powerful crusader kingdom rivaling Jerusalem.

Following the debacle, Emperor Conrad returned to his country via Constantinople with his remaining forces, while King Louis VII remained in Jerusalem until the spring of 1149 AD before departing for his kingdom. His delay was prompted by his intention to divorce his wife, who had dishonored him by engaging in an affair with her uncle, Raymond of Poitiers. The Second Crusade brought about calamities that exacerbated discord among the Crusaders and deepened divisions within Jerusalem itself, particularly between King Baldwin III on one side and his mother and Constable Manasses on the other. Melisende and her adviser suffered losses on multiple fronts, as they missed a significant opportunity to annex Muslim Damascus to Jerusalem and incurred the resentment of other Crusader states in the east, who felt that Jerusalem prioritized its own interests at their expense.

Surprisingly, Queen Eleanor did not return to her county of Aquitaine after her divorce from Louis but instead went to Anjou, where she married Henry, the Duke of Normandy and

Count of Anjou. Henry would soon inherit England after his uncle, King Stephen, who had no heir. Consequently, Eleanor became the Queen of England after being abandoned by the King of France. The Second Crusade presented her with an opportunity to transition from being the Queen of France to becoming the Queen of England.

Two weeks after the debacle of the Second Crusade, King Baldwin III and Constable Manasses engage in a heated private discussion.

King Baldwin III: "Constable Manasses, there is a matter of utmost importance that I must address with you. Over the past six years, since my father's passing, you have been deeply involved in the affairs of the kingdom, offering counsel that has led to nothing but misfortunes. During these years, we witnessed the fall of Edessa to the Muslims, the crumbling of the Crusader states, and the increasing Muslim power under Zengi and his son Nur al-Din. The disaster at Bosra further exposed your shortcomings in governance. And now, we face the unexpected failure of a grand campaign led by the most prominent Western kings in their quest to capture Damascus. What remains for us? Are we to brace ourselves for yet another catastrophe orchestrated by Her Majesty the Queen, influenced by your misguided advice?"

Constable Manasses: "I beg Your Majesty's pardon, but I do not intrude into the kingdom's affairs. Your Majesty and her ladyship the Queen are the sole rulers of this realm, endowed with legitimacy inherited from your grandfather, King Baldwin II. I serve as a mere adviser to your majesties."

King Baldwin III: "You are not just an adviser; you are the architect of schemes within the kingdom. You manipulate my mother to fulfill your desires. You presume the role of the master of God's Kingdom, favored by the Almighty."

Constable Manasses: "Forgive me, Sire. I am your faithful servant, ready to obey your every command. If you wish to dismiss me, I would be honored to continue serving Your Majesty in any capacity, even as your horseman."

King Baldwin III: "Please accept my apologies, Manasses. It was not my intent to offend or belittle you. However, I have come to discuss the impact of your stewardship on the kingdom. It has, regrettably, diminished our prestige both among our Muslim adversaries and our fellow Crusaders."

Constable Manasses: "I remain your loyal servant, committed to following your every directive."

King Baldwin III: "I hope you will continue to serve the kingdom faithfully and adhere to my guidance, without any interference from Her Majesty, the Queen. The affairs of the kingdom should be left to me, as its rightful ruler, to prevent any further damage resulting from misguided administration."

Constable Manasses: "I humbly request your forgiveness for any past advice that may have contributed to the weakening of the kingdom and the loss of its dignity."

King Baldwin III: "It is crucial to acknowledge that both, my mother's governance and your counsel, played a role in the kingdom's decline. Henceforth, I expect you not to involve yourself in the administration of the kingdom. You must inform my mother that you will refrain from meddling in any of the kingdom's affairs. Should I discover any attempt by you to interfere or incite my mother against me, there will be consequences."

Constable Manasses: "Your forgiveness, Sire. Your Majesty is the undisputed ruler of God's Kingdom, and I recognize your unquestionable authority."

King Baldwin III: "It has become evident that you respond best to stern measures. Rest assured, my warnings will not remain mere words. Should you defy me, you will witness them put into action."

Constable Manasses left humiliated after this unexpected encounter that had caught him off guard. He had held the position of royal constable since the onset of Queen Melisende's reign following her husband King Fulk's death in 1143 AD, and he had never anticipated facing such a situation. It became apparent that the young King, at the age of eighteen, aimed to take charge of the kingdom's affairs, even though he had not yet reached the legal age of twenty-one.

Not even a month had passed since the Second Crusade's failure to capture Damascus when Prince Nur al-Din led his troops, joining forces with those from Damascus, and ambushed Prince Raymond de Poitiers' troops. Raymond de Poitiers had departed with only a portion of his forces, failing to wait for the reinforcements on their way to join him. The clash occurred near the fortress of Inab, where the Antioch forces were overwhelmed by the Muslim assault. Raymond himself perished, drenched in his own blood, after putting up a fierce resistance alongside a small group of his soldiers.

Upon receiving news of this latest calamity, King Baldwin III swiftly led his forces to Antioch, fearing its imminent fall to Nur al-Din. Multiple skirmishes unfolded between his troops and those of Nur al-Din until Baldwin III reached Antioch. He entered the city urgently, bolstering the morale of its defenders who had been shaken by their prince's demise. The King personally inspected the state of the defenses before entrusting the guardianship of the ten-year-old Prince Bohemond III to the Patriarch of Antioch. King Baldwin III made this decision independently, without seeking permission from his mother, marking a significant step towards asserting his independence in decision-making. He was motivated by the fear that Antioch might suffer the same fate as Edessa had six years earlier, falling into Muslim hands due to the actions of his mother and Constable Manasses.

However, the Patriarch of Antioch had an intriguing plan. He sent word to Joscelin II, Count of the remnants of Edessa, who had established a temporary capital in Tell Bashir, urging him to abandon his post and join him in Antioch, where he would become the guardian of Prince Bohemond III, the son of his late rival, Raymond of Poitiers. What the Patriarch did not know was that Princess Constance, the mother of Bohemond III, had different intentions. As soon as Princess Constance learned of this arrangement, she secretly informed the Muslims about Joscelin II's impending arrival. They ambushed him on his way to Antioch, and he fell into Nur al-Din's hands in Aleppo. This turn of events left what remained of Edessa's county in the hands of Beatrice, Joscelin II's wife, who became the guardian of their young son, Joscelin III. Consequently, Antioch came under the rule of Princess Constance as the guardian of her son Bohemond III, while the remnants of Edessa's county were under Beatrice's authority as the guardian of her minor son Joscelin III. The Crusader historian William of Tyre described the situation in these two states, both under female governments, as "a divine punishment for the sins of the Crusaders." He wrote that "God had withdrawn guidance from their princes and left them to fend for themselves under the rule of women."

In the year 1150 AD, Baldwin III, the King of Jerusalem, embarked on a grand ambition. He initiated the restoration of a portion of the city of Gaza, located ten miles south of Ascalon. His goal was to transform it into a fortress capable of posing a continuous threat to the Muslim city of Ascalon, with the intention of eventually conquering it. He entrusted the Templars, the holy knights, with the defense and strategic use of Gaza to weaken Ascalon. Ascalon was the last coastal city still under the control of Fatimid Egypt.

By 1151 AD, Baldwin III had reached the legal age of twenty-one to rule the kingdom. He decided to crown himself without the presence of his mother, Queen Melisende, despite the counsel of the Patriarch of Jerusalem, who feared that this would strain the relationship between the King and his mother, who was also his co-ruler. The coronation occurred without the knowledge or attendance of the queen, who realized that her son was moving towards sole rule of the kingdom. She had always considered herself not just as a guardian but as a partner in authority ever since her father, Baldwin II, had crowned her two decades earlier before his passing.

After Baldwin III's self-coronation, he dispatched his adviser, Humphrey of Toron, with a straightforward message to his mother. He proposed dividing the kingdom between them, as it had never been governed by two co-rulers with separate authority before.

A candid conversation unfolds between Queen Melisende and Humphrey in the presence of Constable Manasses.

Constable Manasses: "You have ignited the flames of resentment in the King's heart against his mother, the Queen, and led him to crown himself without her by his side, depriving her of the moment she had longed for, to see her son come of age to rule the kingdom."

Humphrey: "His Majesty the King is not a marionette whose strings his leaders pull. He is a grown man who makes choices and accepts full accountability. He made this choice himself, and no one pushed him to do so."

Queen Melisende: "Yes... He is indeed a chooser, a daring one, but also a disrespectful one. That is not how I raised him. He may have picked up such behavior from the foes of the kingdom, like you, Humphrey."

Humphrey: "Pardon me, Your Majesty. I hope you can maintain harmony between you and your son, His Majesty the King. His Majesty still holds deep love and respect for you, as you are his mother who nurtured him with the love of God and instilled in him virtues and manners. For the past eight years, Your Majesty governed the kingdom independently with the advice of Constable Manasses, without facing any opposition from His Majesty. However, now that he has reached maturity, he wishes to take on real responsibility. He proposes to Your Majesty to divide the kingdom between you both fairly, to avoid any strife that could endanger the bond and love between mother and son. His proposal is that his portion encompasses all the coastal cities, from Tyre to Acre, while Jerusalem, Nablus, and their dependencies remain under your rule."

The Queen let out a piercing shriek: "Woe to me! Woe to me! God's Kingdom is crumbling and losing its glory due to the ambitions of a child. All the blood that was spilled and all the souls that were sacrificed to build and protect it... all going to waste! How I wish not to live to witness the day when I see God's Kingdom torn apart by traitors like you, Humphrey, and your vile associates who corrupted my kind son... God's curse on everyone who tore God's kingdom asunder... God's curse..."

Humphrey: "Forgive me, Your Majesty. I do not utter a word without His Majesty's consent, as he is the one who has given me this command. Neither I nor any of the kingdom's leaders, whom you accuse of treason, have the authority to divide the kingdom. We are all faithful servants of God's Kingdom. The true traitors are those who mismanaged the kingdom over the past eight years with their poor performance and counsel... My lord did not send me here to engage in contentious debates with Your Majesty but only to obtain your signature on this document, by which you agree to the division ordered by His Majesty. This arrangement is intended for the common good."

Queen Melisende: "A scheme that you hatched in secret with the haughty child who was deluded, thinking that leading the kingdom's army in several campaigns, with my approval, gave him command authority. You have severed the bond between me and my son. God's curse be upon you, O minions of Satan, O those who delight in sowing discord among loved ones. You have torn me away from my son, and today, you tear God's Kingdom apart, O enemies of the Lord. God's curse be upon you."

Humphrey: "I implore Your Majesty to sign this document and I deeply display my thanks. I apologize for presenting this challenging request to Your Majesty, but His Majesty's order is mandatory, and he insists on enforcing it out of dire necessity."

The Queen snatched the document fiercely, and with a heart full of sorrow, she signed the paper that tore the Kingdom of God apart, all the while yelling at Humphrey's face: "God will judge you, O enemy of God… God's curse on you all, O traitors."

Humphrey took the document, then whispered to the Constable a verbal threat from the King, warning him of disobedience, making his blood run cold and his face turn pale. He warned him not to oppose this agreement between the King and his mother; otherwise, he would face a different kind of reckoning, one that only he knows, since he had witnessed the consequences of the King's rage and fury. Then Humphrey left, apologizing to Her Majesty for what she had to do against her will, and assured her that he was merely a faithful servant to His Majesty King Baldwin III. He glanced at the Constable Manasses with disdain, then departed, cunningly feigning respect for the Queen. And thus, the Crusader Kingdom of Jerusalem was split up, by an unprecedented agreement in Crusader history in the East, not by the hands of its Muslim enemies, but its Crusader rulers themselves. But it is arguable that this perilous step was the inevitable end of the road previous King Baldwin II had paved with his decision to share the ruling of the kingdom with his daughter Melisende. This division established the principle that says the impossibility of a successful dual rule of the kingdom by two rulers, the King and his mother.

The division document was signed, and Humphrey was appointed as Constable and commander-in-chief of the army by a decree issued by the King. This Humphrey was the owner of Toron Castle and other fiefs near Tyre. He was the most loyal leader to the King.

King Baldwin III was not satisfied with Constable Manasses following the orders and honoring the division agreement. Instead, he insisted on getting rid of him, depriving him of his many fiefs in the kingdom, and stripping him of all influence in the lands under his mother's authority in Jerusalem, Nablus, and their surroundings. Therefore, the King took advantage of Manasses' presence in Mirabel Castle and besieged him there. Manasses quickly surrendered and gave up what he owned in Palestine, particularly in the region east of the Dead Sea. Then the King marched with his forces to Nablus and easily took control of it. However, he was still not satisfied with this coercion and carried out a much bolder and adventurous move. He marched with his forces to Jerusalem itself to subdue it, along with his mother, who had fortified herself there.

He was able to win over many of his mother's followers with promises and threats. Only her son Amalric, Count of Jaffa, Philip of Nablus, Rorhard le Grand, and a few others remained loyal to her. When Queen Melisende learned that her son had marched with his forces to seize her only city, Jerusalem, she became furious and decided to confront her rebellious son herself. She led the fierce battle without resorting to her many leaders who did not dare to confront the King. She fortified herself in the Holy City with her faithful followers and challenged her son's audacity and rudeness. Patriarch Fulk tried to make a last attempt to sway the King from his determination to seize the city by force and prevent bloodshed, especially since the Queen's life was at stake. He attempted to persuade the King to abide by the terms of the agreement he had signed with his mother, so that she could live in peace with what remained of her possessions, according to the agreement, but the King would not budge.

The defenders of the city opened the gates of the Holy City to spare bloodshed, and the King entered with his forces. However, the Queen insisted on her position to break her son's siege and fortified herself with what remained of her loyalists in the castle. It was as if she was dealing with her arch-enemy. The King poured out his anger on the castle, his mother, and those who stood with her in a fierce, continuous attack with catapults during a merciless fight. It seemed that his rage toward his mother and her aides had reached its limit, and the constant bombardment continued on the castle for several days, but she would not surrender. Then mediators intervened, convincing the Queen reluctantly to give up all her possessions except Nablus, which was her dowry that she received when she married King Fulk. Thus, blood was saved at the last moment, and the King ruled the United Kingdom for the first time alone, without his mother's dispute.

And so, after months of strife and bloodshed, the Crusader kingdom in the East was once again whole. The King had made his mother's followers quake in their boots with his threats and had bought their loyalties with promises and intimidation. The Queen, who had witnessed the horror of shells raining down on her palace for days, finally saw the error of her ways. She had ruled the kingdom with tyranny, enjoying giving orders to the leaders, spending time with whomever she fancied among them, and watching them carry out her orders. But now, her son had snatched away her power and glory.

With an iron fist, King Baldwin III showed that he was fit to rule the kingdom by himself and that he was ready to face the dangers that had plagued it because of his mother's mismanagement during her years of tyranny with the help of Manasses, who had run the kingdom into the ground when the threats against it were mounting. This was especially concerning with the rise of Islamic unity led by the Muslim prince, Nur al-Din of Aleppo. Nur al-Din was then looking to reunite his father's state and annex Damascus to it, forming an Islamic force to liberate the Muslim lands that the Crusaders had occupied in the East. This was what King Baldwin III had feared even before he rebelled against his mother and took over the kingdom in the year 1151 AD. After becoming the sole ruler of the kingdom, he set out to solve the problems that his mother had left behind, most importantly, what to do with what was left of the county of Edessa.

This dialogue takes place between King Baldwin III and his army commander Constable Humphrey.

Constable Humphrey: "My lord, we have received a letter from Countess Beatrice, guardian of her son Count Joscelin III. She says that the Byzantine Emperor Manuel has made her an offer she cannot refuse, which is to buy what remains of her county for a handsome sum and take it over to protect it from the Muslims who are trying to seize it, especially Mas'ud, King of Seljuk Rum, and Nur al-Din of Aleppo, our sworn enemy."

King Baldwin III: "We have a real problem on our hands. It started seven years ago when we lost the city of Edessa due to our negligence and escalated when we allowed the feud between Joscelin II and the late Prince of Antioch, Raymond de Poitiers, to spiral out of control. To make matters worse, my mother and the infamous Manasses did not take the matter of this county seriously, allowing power-hungry schemers to run amok and fight over its leadership. It began with Princess Constance, the mastermind behind Joscelin II's capture by Prince Nur al-Din. She did not appreciate his meddling in the guardianship of her underage son, Bohemond III, and sought to have the upper hand in ruling the state by becoming his sole guardian. Today, I have taken charge of the kingdom, but, as fate would have it, I lack the strength to hold onto the fortresses of Tell Bashir, Aintab, Semesat, and others, which are all that remains of Edessa. This is especially true since Muslim leaders Prince Nur al-Din and King Mas'ud are closing in, seeking to claim what remains of this beleaguered county."

Constable Humphrey: "A beleaguered county indeed. Even the Emperor of Germany and the King of France referred to it as a forgotten county when they came three years ago on their Second Crusade to the East, turning a deaf ear to our pleas for help in restoring the city, which was their alleged campaign goal. Furthermore, its people are at each other's throats. The Latins do not trust the Armenians, and the Armenians do not trust the Latins. We Latins have betrayed the Armenians by failing to grant them the powers and privileges we promised if they joined forces with us against our Muslim foes during the first campaign."

King Baldwin III: "I believe we should accept Emperor Manuel's offer. While I know he may not be able to protect the remnants of the county from Muslim threats, I would rather see the county in Byzantine hands when it falls to the Muslims than risk losing it while it is under our control. It is a difficult decision to relinquish this county, one that my grandfather Baldwin II worked hard to preserve. He ruled over it before ascending to the throne in 1118 AD. I wish circumstances were different and that I didn't have to make this choice. That wretched Manasses lost this county, failing to recognize its significance as the first city to embrace Christianity, even before Emperor Constantine the Great's conversion in 312 AD through the famous Milan decree. Despite all this, I will personally lead our forces and hand over what remains of the county to the Byzantines."

And so, the King led his forces, along with those of Tripoli commanded by Count Raymond II, and they surrendered these fortresses to the Byzantines.

In a pitiful and heart-wrenching scene, the people of the county, both Latins and Armenians, who refused to live under Byzantine authority and preferred to remain in the Kingdom of Jerusalem, departed from their lost county under the escort of knights. Weeping and wailing, they carried all their belongings and mourned the fate of their county.

And thus, the Crusader County of Edessa was erased from the map of the Crusader entity, both geographically and politically, returning to Islamic sovereignty after fifty-five years since its establishment. What remained of it, taken by the Byzantines, would eventually be lost to the Muslims, whether to Prince Nur al-Din, the Artuqids, or the King of Seljuk Rum.

King Baldwin III was now relieved of the burden of Edessa and could turn his attention to the new problems left by his mother, the Queen, and her advisor Constable Manasses.

After Edessa crumbled and disintegrated, a meeting took place between Queen Melisende and Constable Manasses in Nablus, which was all that remained for her of her fief after she lost her authority over the kingdom by a violent military coup carried out by the King as previously mentioned. The meeting was arranged in secret, since the King has warned Manasses from interfering in the affairs of the kingdom or meeting with the Queen.

Queen Melisende: "I see signs of a grand plan that His Majesty the King has in the works, aimed at restoring the kingdom's dignity and unity to the days of his grandfather, Baldwin II. May God have mercy on your soul, O father, Baldwin of Bourg. You devoted yourself to the prosperity of the Kingdom of God, giving your all to keep it cohesive and united. Your clever, calculated moves will never be forgotten, such as marrying your daughter Alice to Prince Bohemond II of Antioch, thus securing your control over Antioch. You also managed to influence your cousin Joscelin de Courtenay, granting him the county of Edessa, ensuring his loyalty and submission. You even secured your own coronation as King of the Kingdom of God in 1118 AD, with the consensus of the kingdom's dignitaries, and you effectively subdued the Count of Tripoli with an iron hand. However, alas, your foolish grandson is on the verge of losing your city, Edessa, without comprehending its great value and significance. It was a city you established alongside your cousin Baldwin of Boulogne during the early days of the Holy Pilgrimage called for by Pope Urban II."

Constable Manasses: "Do not blame His Majesty the King, my lady. He is surrounded by counselors who justify these actions for him with strange arguments. If only we had protected the county of Edessa before it fell into Muslim hands in 1144 AD, it all started to go downhill from there. Even after that, if we had seized the opportunity to assist Count Joscelin II when he reclaimed it in 1146 AD after defeating Christianity's enemy, Zengi, his son Nur al-Din, our arch-nemesis, might not have succeeded in defeating and killing Prince Raymond de Poitiers of Antioch. But that was just the beginning; he ordered his forces to invade Antioch, and by then, it was too late. No one could stop him. If only we could return to the days when we led the kingdom, we might restore the dignity and honor of the Kingdom of God to its glorious reign."

Queen Melisende: "Yes, we ruled with wisdom, prudence, and power. But it was the personal enmity between Prince Raymond de Poitiers and Count Joscelin II that cost us Edessa's city. Their greed to exploit the Second Crusade for their personal benefit, and their refusal to participate in it, wasted its chance of success!"

Constable Manasses: "Yes, my lady, we ruled with a strong hand and a firm grip. We even made the bold move of annexing Bosra and Saruj to the Kingdom of God when our friend Altuntash presented us with these two fortresses! The failure of the military campaign and the King's lack of courage in storming Bosra were among the causes of its failure. Indeed, we were unrivaled leaders! But our enemies begrudged us and foiled our project of annexing the Muslim state of Damascus to our kingdom when the French King and German Emperor came to us with the greatest armies of the West. May God condemn the enemies of the Kingdom of God who squandered this great opportunity!"

Queen Melisende: "Have we not cursed people enough? We have given them a tongue-lashing, but it is we who got disgraced. Here I am, a queen with no authority over anything except the wretched city of Nablus. I have lost my dignity and prestige among the leaders of the kingdom. They no longer compete to show me their obedience and submission. Gone are the days of glory when I gave orders to the leaders who humbled themselves before my greatness. How I wish those days would come back, days when all the leaders kissed my hand, when I felt the peace of mind and harmony with my sons, the leaders of the kingdom."

Constable Manasses: "Excuse me, Your Majesty the Queen, for I am your loyal servant. If you want me to kiss your hand, I will do so in a heartbeat!"

Queen Melisende: "It seems you misunderstood me. You thought I enjoyed humiliating my people when all I want is to be surrounded by people showing their love and appreciation for me. But now, I am nothing but a queen who has lost her grace. Only recognized as queen by you, you miserable advisor."

Constable Manasses: "Excuse me, my lady. I did not mean to offend Your Majesty. You are still the revered Queen in the eyes of the people. They still see you as their lady and the daughter of our lord, His Majesty King Baldwin II."

Queen Melisende: "How I wish I could believe this, but only a few months ago, I saw them willingly open the gates of the Holy City to my ungrateful son's army and abetting his humiliation of me in the castle of the city. Shells were pouring down on my head like raindrops. I can almost still hear the horrible sound of shelling that made my heart almost escape my chest. I am no longer a ruler but by title. I am the Queen who was sold by her subjects for a song. I became the outcast. The days of honor are gone, and the days of disgrace have come."

Constable Manasses: "It seems that you have a heavy heart, Your Majesty. I wish I could bring back those glories for Your Majesty, but that is beyond my capabilities since your son turned against us. He stripped me of all my fiefs and warned me against any interference in the affairs of the kingdom. Nothing remained for Your Majesty except Nablus. The days of power are gone, and the days of regret have come."

Queen Melisende: "On a different note, I see that our rebel wants to wash his hands of bearing responsibility for ruling Antioch and protecting it, especially since our enemy Nur al-Din's threat on it has grown more dangerous. He seized important fortresses near its capital, Antioch, like Harim, which is only ten miles away from it. Our ungrateful King wants to marry Antioch's Princess Constance to one of his close commanders so he can secure the state's loyalty to him. But I will do my best to convince my niece, Constance, to remain a widow and keep her independence, just as I did since I was bereaved by my dear husband Fulk's sudden, tragic death nine years ago when he fell from his horse and hit his saddle. I chose to devote myself to raising my brat of a son, Baldwin, and Amalric, the dutiful one. Meanwhile, this poor Constance was bereaved by her father Bohemond II's death when she was only a child of no more than five years old, and her mother Alice was all she had left. Then Antioch's patriarch wronged her and wedded her to Prince Raymond de Poitiers when she was a nine-year-old child, trapping her in a world she did not even understand nor choose, and denying her the innocence of childhood. As if that poor soul had not suffered enough, death took her husband when he was fighting our enemy Nur al-Din three years ago. She deserves to finally enjoy the freedom that she was deprived of as a child."

Constable Manasses: "Yes, my lady, Princess Constance should have the freedom to choose the right man to marry. I suggest that she marry an older man who appreciates her beauty and youth, just as Your Majesty did when you married His Majesty King Fulk."

Queen Melisende: "Yes, my choice was wise, even though those who tried to turn King Fulk against me soured it. They accused my honorable cousin, Hugh, of conspiring against the King and tried to kill him. He died affected by the wounds they inflicted on him, God have mercy on him, during his journey back to the West after he was betrayed in the East. If only he had been alive now that my husband, King Fulk, is dead, for I would have taken him as my personal advisor and commander of the kingdom's army instead of you, Sir Manasses!"

Constable Manasses: "The Lord works in mysterious ways, taking the virtuous and the devout to His side and leaving the wretched ones like myself behind, allowing me to climb to that lofty position that I relished for eight years until your son tore it from my grasp for good. But back to the subject at hand, I hope that Princess Constance finds the right spouse who will bring her joy and safeguard the state from the peril of the enemies."

Queen Melisende: "I will not let that ingrate wretch savor his reign, for I will not allow him to marry her to one of his leaders. Instead, I will keep him preoccupied with the matter of Antioch throughout his rule and make him taste the bitterness of controlling this state, with our Byzantine brothers on his heels, more eager to dominate it than our Muslim enemies themselves. It is home to the great church that bears the name of the chief of Christ's disciples, Saint Peter. How I wish to wed Constance to a reckless leader who would drag my ingrate into a dispute with the Byzantine Emperor Manuel, who has always favored the Latins more than any other Greek emperor since the days of his grandfather Alexios Komnenos, who beckoned us about fifty-nine years ago to help him against the Muslims. We came with our mighty armies and built the Kingdom of God in the East. I wish I could see that ingrate taste the bitterness of a conflict with the Byzantines."

Months after this exchange, the King pays a visit to his mother in her fiefdom in Nablus, where he apologizes to her for his ill conduct, expressing regret for spurning her kindness and dishonoring her. The incident occurred after he rained down catapults on her castle in Jerusalem, where she sought refuge last year. It was when he coerced her to renounce the rule of the kingdom, leaving her only Nablus and its lands. After many mediations were offered to the Queen, she agreed to listen to his apology, but one that would suit Her Majesty's honor and balance out the enormity of the affront she endured from him. During the meeting, the Queen showed up scowling furiously at her son.

This meeting and dialogue takes place between King Baldwin III and his mother Queen Melisende in private.

King Baldwin III: "I express my sincere remorse, for I have gravely wronged Your Majesty—the mother of mercy, the tender one, with a heart of gold, a heart vast enough to embrace every ungrateful son of the kingdom, not just me. I wish I had never seen the light of day, so as not to witness the day I rebelled against the one who nurtured me with love, tolerance, and compassion. But my wicked soul and evil counselors tempted me to use force against Your Majesty."

Queen Melisende: "I wish the words you have just uttered came from a sincere and repentant heart. Alas, they emanate from a black, cold heart, from a man who seeks his own interests even at the cost of cruelty to his own mother, one who nurtured him with mercy and kindness. I never imagined that you would go so far as to commit such wicked acts against any of your subjects, let alone against your merciful mother—the rightful heir of the kingdom, crowned by your grandfather Baldwin II with his own hands."

King Baldwin III: "You still hold the power and remain the revered Queen in the Kingdom of God. I will abide by your every command, no matter what it may be. Your orders are to be executed without question, for I have been blessed to have you as my mother. Your favor upon me never wanes as long as my heart beats, and your blessings have brought glory and prosperity to the kingdom."

Queen Melisende: "Sweet words will not alter reality. Today, you are the acknowledged king, and neither I nor anyone else can object to your commands. You have come to apologize a year after your heinous act, seeking my help for some purpose that would strengthen your tenuous legitimacy, acquired through the sword and the catapults that rained upon my palace, and by swaying the consciences of the kingdom's army leaders who forsook their oath of allegiance to me in favor of you."

King Baldwin III: "All the leaders and soldiers of the kingdom are obedient to Your Majesty, including your humble servant and your wayward son who has come to seek his Mistress's pardon and forgiveness."

Queen Melisende: "My heart still bears the weight of your actions, even a year later. Your sweet words and false pleas cannot heal the wounds you have inflicted. You excel at playing the role of a contrite penitent, appearing as a harmless sheep but, in reality, a hungry wolf waiting for an opportunity to strike."

King Baldwin III: "I will not cease in seeking your forgiveness, not until the day I depart this world, O most merciful mother. Your wise words and guidance are deeply embedded within me, like a guiding light that leads me on the path of righteousness. I need you and your blessings now more than ever."

Queen Melisende: "You can beg and plead for forgiveness, and feign submission all day, but you must know that it makes no difference to me. None of it matters now that you have stripped me of all power. The only thing left for me from ruling is the title of a queen, without a say or opinion in the matters of her kingdom. You have taken away my power, along with the respect of my people, who rebelled against me, disgracing and stripping me of my dignity. The great leaders used to be eager to have the honor of meeting me and discussing important matters of the kingdom. They were keen on seeking my advice on every matter."

King Baldwin III: "If the leaders were keen on seeking your advice, then I, today, am the most eager of all for my dear mother's guidance. Your Majesty, you are the revered queen, and I would be honored if you could advise me on the matter of marrying Princess Constance to one of the competent leaders so that he can take care of Antioch's affairs. With my limited capabilities, I fear I may not be able to manage Antioch as my grandfather Baldwin of Bourg did."

Queen Melisende: "Why not consider getting married yourself, rather than involving yourself in the marriage of your cousin's daughter and Antioch's affairs? You are now twenty-three years old and haven't given marriage a thought. However, it seems you prefer to spend your time corrupting the wives of your leaders, those who supported the coup against me and stripped me of my power."

King Baldwin III: "I was raised in the warmth of your embrace, where you instilled chastity and honor in me, especially after my father's death when I was only thirteen years old. You set an example of a chaste and modest life and even arranged for chaste women to teach me lessons in modesty and virtue. Look at the fruit of your splendid efforts in raising and nurturing me."

Queen Melisende: "You ungrateful child! Has your arrogance blinded you to forget who you are addressing? I am the Queen, an embodiment of high morals and ethics. I raised you to be well-mannered with everyone, yet here you stand, rude and disrespectful to your own mother! You ungrateful wretch! You dare to hurl insults and accusations at me. You have confirmed my suspicion – you have not changed. You are still the ungrateful son with a sharp tongue. You have crossed the line of impudence, accusing me of being the reason you behave immorally and tarnish people's honor. May God condemn you, you enemy of God, pretending to rule the Kingdom of God, when you are barely worthy of ruling the kingdom of the devil."

King Baldwin III: "I apologize to Your Majesty for my slip of the tongue. I misspoke, and I am not without sins. I have my weaknesses and make mistakes, but I know that God will forgive me, for I have an innocent heart and pure intentions."

The King takes his mother's hand and presses his lips against it in utter humiliation and deep regret for what he said to her with his insolence and disrespect. After much reproach and scolding, she accepts his apology despite herself, fearing a new offense. She found herself forced to stay on good terms with her son since all aspects of power now lay in his hands. After many attempts to convince her, she agreed to persuade her niece, Princess Constance, to marry one of the leaders. She also consented to attend a special meeting that would be held in the city of Tripoli, hosted by her sister, Countess Hodierna, wife of Count Raymond II of Tripoli. During the meeting, the Queen would convince Constance to choose one of the leaders that the King would present to her.

On the day of the meeting, a candid exchange takes place between those present.

King Baldwin III: "It is my honor to present to you three of the finest leaders of the kingdom for Princess Constance to choose from as a husband, to be her assistant and consultant in managing the affairs of the state. This role requires the competence and courage of one of these brave leaders. Each of them hails from noble families and lineages that befit the princess's sovereignty and her noble family, as a descendant of Prince Bohemond II, son of Bohemond I, and grandson of Robert Guiscard, whose name reached the heavens. These leaders also have a long history of governance and management, as well as experience in dealing with the dangers we face due to the growing threat of our fierce enemy, Nur al-Din of Aleppo, who killed Prince Raymond de Poitiers, the late husband of Princess Constance, four years ago."

Countess Hodierna: "I would like to begin by welcoming you all to the County of Tripoli, a brave city that has stood strong in the face of all threats, unafraid of powerful enemies lurking like predators. This county embodies dignity, freedom, and independence. It has always been a staunch ally of the kingdom, led by King Baldwin III, in our shared pursuit of a future marked by peace and prosperity. As Princess Constance's aunt, I endorse the King's proposal and implore Princess Constance to choose one of these distinguished leaders for the important task. She should agree to have him as her husband and partner in governing the state, as well as a guardian for Prince Bohemond III, the son of Raymond de Poitiers."

Princess Constance: "I thank His Majesty the King for his proposal and all of you for your concern regarding the protection of my state against the menace of our foes. However, as you all know, it has been only four years since I lost my beloved husband, Prince Raymond de Poitiers. I am still deeply grieved by his departure, just as much as the day it happened. His beautiful memory lives on in my heart and mind. He filled the void left by the absence of my father, Prince Bohemond II, who was killed by our enemies when I was just a child of five. Then, when I was only nine, King Fulk, the father of His Majesty King Baldwin III, wed me to the late Prince Raymond. From that union, I bore three children, among them Prince Bohemond III, who is now eleven years old. He, along with his sisters Marie and Philippa, needs my tender care to compensate for the loss of their father. I do not wish to marry now, as it may lead to neglecting these children."

Queen Melisende: "I would like to express my appreciation for the King's dedication to preserving the Kingdom of God, which my father, King Baldwin II, entrusted me with, along with my husband, King Fulk, and the current King, who was but a one-year-old infant at the time. I guarded it with King Fulk until his death in 1143 AD. Afterward, I worked tirelessly with the leaders of the kingdom to protect and shield it until the ominous year of 1151 AD, when I was dishonored and denied my power and authority by my ungrateful son. However, let us set personal disputes aside. I agree with him and stand by his proposal to marry my dear Constance to one of these competent leaders."

King Baldwin III: "I would like to reiterate my gratitude to all of you, especially Her Majesty the Queen, who ruled the kingdom with unwavering strength and power. She instilled fear in the hearts of our enemies and made them think twice before threatening the Kingdom of God. During her blessed era, she sought to expand the Kingdom of God to encompass new lands. When the Second Crusade came after losing Edessa to Zengi, the enemy of Christianity, Her Majesty the

Queen attempted to annex the Muslim state of Damascus to the Kingdom of God. Unfortunately, the plots of our enemies thwarted the campaign and wasted the opportunity for the Kingdom of God. In the spirit of continuing Her Majesty's efforts to preserve the Kingdom of God, I hope that Princess Constance will accept one of these gallant men as her husband to assist her in upholding the independence of Antioch."

Princess Constance: "I have already expressed how deeply sorrow fills my heart since parting with Prince Raymond, and I am not prepared for marriage now. I beg you to spare me from it. I have endured much since childhood; you have meddled enough in shaping my life. You married me off when I was a child of nine years old, knowing nothing about what marriage entailed. Was it not enough for you, that you now seek to force me into another marriage?"

King Baldwin III: "We do not intend to coerce you into anything; it is merely a suggestion. If you insist on not marrying, that is your decision. However, we urge you to consider marriage for the sake of preserving the state, given the mounting threat of our enemy Nur al-Din. If only I had the strength to manage the state alongside my duty of overseeing the affairs of the great kingdom."

Countess Hodierna: "I believe we have troubled the noble princess enough. We should grant her the opportunity to ponder marriage if she wishes to do so in the future."

King Baldwin III: "I welcome the idea; she should indeed take the time to contemplate the matter. I appreciate all of you for attending this meeting. I hope we can convene more often in the future to unite our forces and serve our common interest, that of the Kingdom of God."

The meeting adjourned, and the king's aspirations were dashed. The Queen, however, was delighted. She had been a snake in the grass to her son since he had robbed her of her rightful throne. She had pretended to support the King's idea of Constance's marriage while secretly poisoning Constance's mind against it. This meeting appeared to be the spark that ignited a feud between Countess Hodierna and her husband, Raymond II, Count of Tripoli. The exact event that triggered this quarrel remained unknown, but it was fierce. It escalated to the point where Hodierna called for her sister, Queen Melisende, to come to Tripoli to help mediate, but their efforts failed to resolve the dispute. Consequently, Hodierna decided to accompany Queen Melisende to Nablus and stay there until the storm passed. Raymond II had no choice but to allow her to leave. As he escorted her outside the city walls, he met his tragic fate at the hands of assassins, who then escaped. The Crusaders blamed the assassins for this murder, an Ismaili sect that had split from mainstream Ismaili doctrine and adopted assassination as a means of advancing their influence and goals. The Crusaders often accused them of assassinating their leaders. However, it is possible that Raymond II's death was plotted by his wife, Hodierna, and perhaps with the involvement of her sister, Queen Melisende.

When King Baldwin III learned of Raymond II's death, he promptly led his forces to Tripoli. He restored order to the city, which had been in turmoil following its ruler's assassination. People had indiscriminately attacked anyone who was not Latin, including the local Maronite Christians, seeking vengeance for their ruler's death based on unfounded accusations. It is possible that they were unaware that those who benefited most from arranging the Count's murder were his wife, Hodierna, and her sister, Queen Melisende. Hodierna wanted unrestricted control over ruling the county as the guardian of her twelve-year-old son, Raymond III. Queen Melisende, on the other hand, reveled in exacerbating her son the King's troubles, keeping him occupied with Tripoli, much as she had done with Antioch before. Thus, Hodierna assumed guardianship over her son, Raymond III, who had yet to come of age.

Thus, another Crusader entity in the East was now under a woman's authority. Even though Queen Melisende had lost her voice in leading the kingdom a year ago, her sister Countess Hodierna now controlled Tripoli. Antioch was under her niece Constance's authority through guardianship over her son Bohemond III. Edessa had been erased from the political map after a woman took charge of it, namely Beatrice, following her husband Joscelin II's capture four years ago in 1148 AD. Only Jerusalem remained under a man's rule. If King Baldwin III were to be killed, his brother Amalric would succeed him under the guardianship of their mother, Queen Melisende. Thus, effectively, all Crusader entities would be ruled by women. It seemed that these women inherited their mother, Queen Morphia's, Armenian origin love for control and aspirations to extend their authority over the Crusader entity, asserting themselves in its rule. It can be argued that Queen Morphia's marriage to King Baldwin of Burg back when he was Count of Edessa in 1102 AD had a ripple effect, gradually leading them to involve themselves more in governing the Crusader states, ultimately weakening the entity.

The city of Jerusalem faced a grave Islamic threat from Turkish Muslim factions led by the Artuqids, who had once ruled the Holy Land under the Seljuk Sultan Malik Shah before the Crusades began a few years later. They had now carved out their own domain in the northeast of the Fertile Crescent in Diyarbakir. King Baldwin III managed to thwart this threat by ambushing the Muslim forces as they marched from Jericho to the Jordan River. He routed them with his forces, and they retreated in defeat, leaving about five thousand men dead or wounded. The Crusader forces from Tripoli also harassed them as they fled across the rapids of the Jordan River, adding to their losses. Thus, King Baldwin III demonstrated his skill and resolve in facing this threat in a record time of no more than one day, which was the thirteenth of November in 1152 AD. It marked the ninth year of his reign under his mother's guardianship and the second year since his coronation and taking over the kingdom, after stripping his mother of her legitimacy.

With the dawn of the next year in January 1153 AD, King Baldwin III took a bold step by attempting to capture the last Islamic port in the Levant, Ascalon. None of the Crusader leaders had made any serious efforts to seize this strategic city that separated the Crusader Kingdom of Jerusalem from Fatimid Egypt. Had the Crusaders been able to occupy it, it would have paved the way for their conquest of Fatimid Egypt, which was weak at that time. King Baldwin III summoned all the Crusader forces to help him tighten the siege on the city, both by land and sea. New Crusaders who had arrived in the East as pilgrims also joined them and volunteered to contribute to the siege. The King spared no expense to carry out this grand operation.

In the fourth month of the siege, Reynald de Chatillon approached the King in the Crusader camp besieging Ascalon, seeking his approval to marry Princess Constance. The princess had sent this relatively unknown knight to obtain the King's personal approval because she was a vassal of the King. Here, we are drawn to the King's haste in agreeing to this marriage, which would later have negative consequences for the Crusader entity. Reynald was a knight who lacked chivalrous qualities, making this marriage a calamity for Antioch and its princess who had refused to marry one of the three finest Crusader knights just a year ago. However, now she agreed to wed a knight who lacked true chivalrous ethics. While the Crusaders as a whole were occupied with the fierce siege of Ascalon, which drained both the defenders and attackers, Constance and Reynald were occupied with their own marriage, which seemed intolerable to delay.

Eight months after the siege had tightened around Ascalon's defenders, they surrendered to King Baldwin III, agreeing to conditions that guaranteed their safety and property. He also provided them with protection until they reached their masters' lands in Egypt safely. The agreement was finalized, and the Crusaders celebrated the acquisition of this great city on the thirteenth of August in the year 1153 AD. The King seized this opportunity to please his mother by granting his brother Amalric, who was loyal to their mother, the city as a fiefdom. Perhaps through this act, he managed to regain some of his mother's favor after insulting her many times before. It is not unlikely that his mother viewed the siege and surrender of Ascalon as an indication that she still had some influence in the kingdom, even if it was symbolic, as all she had left was the title of Her Majesty the Queen.

This dialogue unfolds following the fall of Ascalon and the return of King Baldwin III to Jerusalem with his army commander, Constable Humphrey.

King Baldwin III: "We have accomplished a great feat by capturing this mighty city. Firstly, we have removed a thorn that has been painfully embedded in our side for over fifty years. Moreover, we now share a direct border with the weakened Fatimid Egypt, presenting us with a grand opportunity for invasion, which we must seize. However, we should secure our position in the Levant first and neutralize the threat posed by Nur al-Din. I have heard he is plotting to take over Damascus. If he succeeds and unifies the Levant under his command, it will upset the balance of power and endanger our existence, especially since he has already taken Mosul after his brother Mawdud's death some time ago."

Constable Humphrey: "Indeed, my lord, I find your concern about Nur al-Din's rising power to be well-founded. Although our victory in Ascalon was a glorious achievement for our nation and a splendid moment in your blessed reign, this enemy poses a grave threat to our very existence. Before you ascended to power, we faced one disaster after another under the rule of the infamous Manasses. The menace of Nur al-Din was not taken seriously, and look where it led us. His project to achieve Islamic unity is ambitious, and if he succeeds in annexing Damascus soon, we will not be able to prevent his future ambitions, including annexing Fatimid Egypt. Then, our presence and survival in the East will be in doubt. How I wish for a new crusade from the West to come to our aid and help us annex Damascus to our kingdom before Nur al-Din does. Sadly, our brethren in the West are preoccupied with their own affairs. We dedicate our lives to God's cause while they are absorbed in their worldly interests."

King Baldwin III: "We need practical steps to support our ambitious goals. Perhaps our brethren in the West will view us as more devoted and sincere fighters against our Muslim adversaries now that we have occupied the city of Ascalon. This may motivate them to offer assistance. Nevertheless, we must primarily rely on our own forces. Our Western brethren spared no effort in supporting us during our arduous eight-month siege of Ascalon. During that time, we suffered from shortages of supplies, manpower, and equipment. Waging war against our Muslim adversaries requires substantial funds that we cannot afford. Our enemies, on the other hand, enjoy the support of their homelands and possess deep-seated loyalty to their lands, having lived there for many generations. We, as newcomers to this land for the past fifty-four years, cannot hold it in the same regard as the lands of our Frankish ancestors where we have settled for seven centuries. Despite the initial papal call for the divine quest to occupy the East in the days of Pope Urban II, his successors have been more preoccupied with internal disputes and personal interests than the divine quest. They encourage others to visit Jerusalem, yet they themselves do not undertake such journeys. It is perplexing how the papacy issues orders and then contradicts them. What more can we expect from them?"

Constable Humphrey: "Excellently put, my lord. We must rely on the strength of our own forces rather than wait for the Western kings to come to our aid and resolve our issues. This is especially true considering that they witnessed our internal divisions when they arrived in the East six years ago. The notorious Manasses aimed to manipulate the Second Crusade for his own benefit, to the detriment of other Crusader states, including the County of Edessa, which was the main motivation for coming to the East, as it had fallen to our enemy Zengi ten years prior. This started a chain reaction that brought us to our current situation. Even after the failure to capture Damascus in that crusade, Her Majesty the Queen and Manasses made no effort to reconcile Count Jocelin II of Edessa and his adversary Raymond de Poitiers, the Prince of Antioch, who later perished in battle against our foes five years ago. They were preoccupied with defending Edessa and preventing it from falling into the hands of our nemesis, Nur al-Din Mahmoud, Zengi's son. This led to the need to find a capable prince to lead Edessa, achieved by marrying him to Princess Constance. However, she refused the best candidates from our kingdom and eventually chose Reynald de Chatillon as her spouse. I have concerns about him, as I have heard that he is in conflict with the Patriarch of Antioch and mistreats him. Furthermore, I fear he may strain our relationship with our friend and ally, the Byzantine Emperor Manuel, who has shown us unprecedented respect and support since we arrived in the East on our divine quest during the days of his grandfather, Emperor Alexios Komnenos."

King Baldwin III: "We must bear the consequences of policies that date back to my grandfather Baldwin II's reign. He subjected the Crusader states to political marriages and employed carrot-and-stick policies. Even my late aunt Alice rebelled and defied her father, King Baldwin of Bourg, sending an offer to our enemy Zengi over thirteen years ago, suggesting he take control of Antioch. The troubles continued when my father Fulk married my mother, sparking internal issues, particularly regarding the division of rule after my grandfather's death. My mother also insisted on asserting her authority over my father. Then, after my father's death eleven years ago, my mother ruled the kingdom and acted as my guardian when I was a child. She even attempted to retain her guardianship even after I reached the legal age to rule. I had no choice but to remove her through a tumultuous coup."

Constable Humphrey: "Let us not dwell on the past and the mistakes of our ancestors. They did their best to further the Kingdom of God's goals, even though they made errors. What matters now is correcting those errors. External and internal threats loom over our kingdom, and we must deal with them wisely, avoiding complacency and underestimating their seriousness. Such lapses cost us the County of Edessa and squandered our opportunity to benefit from the Second Crusade."

King Baldwin III: "We will exert ourselves to confront these dangers and elevate our kingdom before it is too late."

Seven months after this meeting, news arrives of Nur al-Din's seizure of the Muslim state of Damascus, a territory the Crusader Kingdom of Jerusalem was very eager to occupy.

This dialogue between King Baldwin III and Constable Humphrey takes place following the spread of this news.

King Baldwin III: "Our worst fear has come true. The people of Damascus surrendered to our enemy Nur al-Din after a short siege and abandoned their prince Mujir al-Din Abaq, who ruled alone after the death of his brilliant Atabeg Unur five years ago. They declared their loyalty to our arch-enemy."

Constable Humphrey: "We mishandled our approach to the affairs of the state of Damascus. For over fifty years, it had been ruled by our allies, who protected their independence against various Muslim powers. This alliance dated back to the days of their grandfather Tughtakin. However, we repaid their loyalty with ingratitude. When the lord of Bosra, Altuntash, rebelled against his master, the Ruler of Damascus eight years ago and offered us his fortresses, we accepted the offer without realizing the grave consequences it could lead to. Then we betrayed our allies again, the rulers of Damascus when we launched the Second Crusade against them five years ago, almost occupying their capital. We cannot expect them to remain in alliance with us, waiting for us to betray them once more or launch a surprise war, perhaps capturing their capital. It seems that they have realized now that the fall of the Fatimid city of Ascalon at our hands seven months ago would hasten the fall of their capital into our hands. So, they chose to hand it over to a strong Muslim leader instead of surrendering to us, as the people of Ascalon did."

King Baldwin III: "After this significant victory for Nur al-Din, where he has occupied the entire state of Damascus, including its cities, fortresses, economic, human, and military resources, he will undoubtedly turn his attention to us, becoming a serious threat to our very existence. This is especially true if he succeeds in seizing Fatimid Egypt. Today, Prince Nur al-Din is hailed as the Just King, having gained the loyalty of many Muslims who view him as a just and courageous ruler, determined to fight and defeat us. His path has been somewhat smoother than his father Zengi's, for he has followed the trail his father blazed. I wish I possessed the power to halt his ambitious expansion. The kingdom's army alone may not be capable of repelling this bold enemy. As for the Antiochene army, it has suffered numerous setbacks in recent years. Then, Reynald de Chatillon arrived and further weakened it, even refusing to join forces with us to confront the looming threat of Nur al-Din. I can almost envision Nur al-Din capturing Reynald, just as he did with Joscelin II, Count of Edessa four years ago, or witnessing Reynald fall by Nur al-Din's hand, as happened to his predecessor Raymond de Poitiers, Prince of Antioch five years ago."

Constable Humphrey: "Your warning to your mother, Queen Melisende, has come true. If she had heeded your advice about the potential consequences of launching the Second Crusade against our ally Damascus five years ago, Nur al-Din wouldn't have emerged as such a formidable threat. His rise to power was facilitated by the failure of the Second Crusade, which led to his leadership of Islamic forces against the Kingdom of God. Now, seven years later, your predictions have become a reality. We can no longer afford to make any missteps. Nur al-Din's ambitions pose a grave threat that cannot be underestimated. Our only viable option is to forge an alliance with the Byzantines. While our Crusader ancestors often viewed the Byzantine emperors with suspicion and dealt with them dishonestly, our choices today are limited. We lack the strength to ensure our survival, and we cannot rely solely on the Latin West and its rulers, who are preoccupied with their own endless problems and conflicts. To that end, I propose that you instruct Reynald de Chatillon, Prince of Antioch and guardian of Bohemond III, to work on improving his relationship with his Byzantine counterparts. This will lay the groundwork for a strong alliance with the Byzantines. Furthermore, when you decide to marry, I recommend that you choose a Byzantine princess. This will provide us with leverage, help cement the alliance, and secure financial support. We are in desperate need of funds to recruit soldiers. The shortage of funds has forced us to cede many of our fortresses to the two factions of the Templars and Hospitallers. Unfortunately, they cannot be fully trusted, as they often prioritize their personal interests over all else. You may recall the incident when we breached the walls of Ascalon weeks before its capture, and the leader of the Templars prevented anyone except his forty soldiers from entering through the breach. He waited until the rest of his men arrived, effectively delaying the city's fall into our hands by several weeks as the defenders of Ascalon regrouped and fortified their defenses."

King Baldwin III: "The papacy has granted these two groups unprecedented privileges and authority in the Kingdom of God, despite their constant internal rivalries and disputes. They continue to expand their influence, and regrettably, we rely on them due to our financial constraints. I share your concerns about the armed monks of these orders, who are often driven by greed, arrogance, and self-interest. Their ongoing disputes with ecclesiastical bishops over tithes, which the papacy has exempted them from, have added to our woes by creating conflicts within the Church. It seems they have embroiled us in new internal problems just as we grapple with external threats. As for my marriage, it remains a private matter for me. I am not prepared to consider it at this time, as my primary focus is on the affairs of the Kingdom of God. I do not want a woman to divert my attention from these responsibilities."

Constable Humphrey: "Your Majesty, I understand that your marriage is a personal matter, but it also has implications for the Kingdom of God and its subjects. If something were to happen to you in these circumstances, your younger brother Amalric might ascend to the throne. He may be influenced by his mother and her policies, which have caused numerous issues for the kingdom and could jeopardize its future."

King Baldwin III: "I appreciate your concern for the Kingdom of God, but I am not currently considering marriage. Perhaps my stance will change in the future, but for now, my focus remains solely on the kingdom."

Constable Humphrey: "I acknowledge your dedication to the kingdom and its affairs, but I hope you have outgrown the follies and indiscretions of youth, including pursuits of romantic dalliances with the beautiful women of the court, which can tarnish your reputation, Your Majesty."

King Baldwin III: "You speak the harsh truth, my friend, and I value your sincere intentions and unwavering loyalty to both me and the Kingdom of God. I must confess that I have struggled with the grip of lust since my father, King Fulk, passed away and my mother assumed control over me. She introduced me to the temptations of courtesans when I was still a boy, and for eight years, she diverted my attention away from ruling the kingdom by ensnaring me in such distractions. Whenever she reprimanded me for indulging with the women of the kingdom, I had to endure her insults, fearing her wrath and her sharp tongue. However, you should be aware that my recklessness with women is a consequence of my mother's actions. She surrounded me with promiscuous women during my formative years, aiming to corrupt my morals and justify her own wicked behavior. It is difficult to imagine any mother actively seeking to ruin her son as mine did. Therefore, when I reached the age of twenty-one and became eligible to rule, my resentment towards her consumed me. I could not contain my anger, and the only way to appease it was by humiliating her. I stripped her of all her powers and possessions, except for her dowry, the city of Nablus. If my mother were ever to revert to her old ways, she and her supporters would face even harsher consequences from me. I harbor no affection for her, and I believe no mother in the world, no matter how wicked, would stoop so low as to derive pleasure from humiliating her son and corrupting his morals to seize power, relishing in the flattery and false respect of men and leaders who flocked to her and kissed her hand. I apologize, my dear Humphrey, for burdening you with my mother's secrets. You are my trusted friend, and I implore you not to disclose this information to anyone."

Constable Humphrey: "Your Majesty, please forgive me. You have poured out your heartfelt emotions, and I am honored that you trust me with your innermost thoughts. I, too, have harbored similar feelings, but I refrained from voicing them to avoid sowing discord among the kingdom's leaders, especially during the reign of the notorious Manasses. However, I am certain that your noble heart is capable of forgiveness, no matter the wrongs done to you, even by your beloved mother. Your Majesty possesses a heart of gold, overflowing with kindness, capable of forgiving offenses even from your enemies, let alone your dear mother. Regarding your request for confidentiality, have you ever known a loyal servant who would betray their master's trust?"

King Baldwin III: "I pray that God will mend the affairs of the kingdom and guide my heart towards the right path while protecting the Kingdom of God."

Two years later, in 1156 AD, an opportunity arose when the Byzantine Emperor sought assistance from Raynald de Chatillon to deal with one of his rebellious Armenian subjects, Thoros. This rebel would frequently raid and pillage the region of Cilicia in southeastern Anatolia before retreating to his mountain fortresses. Emperor Manuel promised Raynald a generous reward for completing this mission. Raynald agreed to the offer and successfully crushed Thoros the Armenian's forces. However, when the promised reward from the Emperor was delayed, Raynald acted impulsively and irresponsibly. He led his forces to the island of Cyprus, which was under the Emperor's control, and engaged in looting and plundering. He went so far as to allow his soldiers to violate the sanctity of monasteries and harm the nuns who were there for worship. Raynald then returned to Antioch, rejoicing in his ill-gotten gains, oblivious to the severity of his actions and the negative impact they would have on relations between the Crusaders and the Byzantines, as well as between the Byzantine Emperor and King Baldwin III.

King Baldwin III and Constable Humphrey of Toron later discusses these recent events.

Constable Humphrey: "Our worst fears regarding this lunatic, whom Princess Constance chose as her spouse and guardian for her son Bohemond III, have become a reality. Just as we are making every effort to appease the Emperor, this fool comes along and disrupts our relationship with him."

King Baldwin III: "I did not anticipate such trouble from Raynald. I knew him as a greedy man who served in my army before he married the princess for a fixed wage and a share of the spoils. I confess that I was mistaken when I hastily consented to the princess's choice of this buffoon as her husband, especially considering her previous rejections of more suitable suitors. But let us not dwell on that now. It is time we take decisive action against this fool before our already strained relations with the Emperor deteriorate further. We have never encountered anyone quite like him among the Byzantine emperors, given his eagerness to befriend us."

Constable Humphrey: "Your Majesty, I believe it would be prudent to dispatch a delegation with a message from you, admonishing this defiant prince and emphasizing the seriousness of his disgraceful actions. We should instruct him to offer a straightforward apology to His Majesty the Emperor."

King Baldwin III: "That is an excellent plan, and I will promptly send the delegation without delay to address the recklessness of this madman. We have endured the errors of others for too long, and we shall continue to suffer as long as we have imprudent leaders like Raynald who disrupt the peace of the Kingdom of God."

The delegation arrives at Raynald de Chatillon's, where they are warmly received. He promises to issue an apology to the Byzantine Emperor but then delays it, unaware that he will one day be compelled to offer an apology that will humiliate not only himself but all the Crusaders.

During the same period, as King Baldwin III's problems mounted, the leader of Islamic unity, the Just King Nur al-

Din, achieved victory after victory. He made peace with his rivals among the Muslim leaders, including Seljuk King of Rum Kilij Arslan II and Seljuk King Alp Arslan, the son of Sultan Mas'ud, whose Atabeg was Zengi, Nur al-Din's own father. At that time, Zengi ruled as the guardian (Atabeg) for King Seljuk Alp Arslan since his father, Seljuk Sultan Mas'ud, had entrusted Zengi with this role when Alp Arslan was a young boy who had not yet reached the legal age to rule.

The year 1157 AD proved to be a peaceful one for the Crusaders in their conflict with the Just King, Nur al-Din, due to a series of earthquakes that struck his kingdom, causing significant damage to many of his fortresses. King Nur al-Din was occupied with the task of repairing these fortresses and reorganizing his military plans.

During this period, the Crusaders completed the construction of a new fortress in the city of Baniyas in 1157 AD. Constable Humphrey encountered significant challenges in providing protection for Baniyas. Consequently, he proposed to King Baldwin III that they enlist the Hospitallers to assist in defending Baniyas, with the understanding that they would be responsible for guarding half of the fortress while the King would defend the other half.

However, when the Hospitaller forces set out for Baniyas on the twenty-sixth of April 1157 AD to assume their duties, they fell into an ambush by Nur al-Din's forces and suffered a devastating defeat, resulting in numerous casualties and prisoners. Following this unfortunate incident, the Hospitallers requested to be exempted from their commitment to defend Baniyas, reneging on the previous agreement.

Subsequently, King Nur al-Din laid siege to Baniyas, and Constable Humphrey and his son displayed remarkable heroism in its defense, despite having only a small number of defenders whose spirits were ignited by the courage shown by the Constable and his son. Baldwin III led his forces to the rescue of Baniyas while it was under siege. Nur al-Din lifted the siege after partially damaging the fortress, which he had managed to control. The Crusader king oversaw the repair and fortification of Baniyas, where only his knights remained. He then advanced with his knights toward Tiberias without taking adequate precautions near Jacob's Ford, where Nur al-Din had set an ambush. An attack by Nur al-Din on the nineteenth of June 1157 AD caused the Crusader forces to scatter. The Crusader King and the remnants of his forces retreated to one of his nearby castles, Safed Castle.

Among the captives taken by Nur al-Din's victorious army were several prominent leaders, including Lord Reynald, the master of the Templar knights. The Crusader King had fallen victim to his own pride and arrogance, misinterpreting Nur al-Din's withdrawal from Baniyas as a sign of fear rather than strategy. He had recklessly left behind his footmen as he hurried back to his throne, creating an opportunity for Nur al-Din to strike with a swift and decisive blow. This catastrophe was a result of the King's own actions, not the actions of others, akin to what Raynald of Antioch had done when he raided the Byzantine Island of Cyprus.

This conversation unfolds between King Baldwin III and Constable Humphrey after the catastrophic incident.

Constable Humphrey: "We have come to know our foe as a mighty warrior who can strike us on many fronts and vanquish us with ease. While we receive one blow after another, we do not seem to heed the lessons of our history."

King Baldwin III: "Indeed, we face a relentless adversary, possessing courage, stamina, and cunning, qualities I wish we had. I made a grave mistake myself when I hastened to disband my footmen and failed to take the appropriate safety measures. We endured that abominable defeat at the hands of our enemy, and we deserved it."

Constable Humphrey: "Indeed, sire, we earned our defeat. Not long ago, we forsook peaceful people in the forests of Baniyas, disregarding their frailty and the vow of protection we had granted them. Our retribution came from our own actions. I pray that we do not commit such a sin again, excusing it with our need for coin. We plundered these feeble ones of their wealth, and God sent us robust men who made us taste the bitterness of defeat and took back what we had plundered from the feeble ones. We are in desperate need of restructuring our forces, providing them with financial backing, and enlisting skilled knights to compensate for the numerical deficiency we suffer from. It is unwise to depend on knights from factions such as the Templars and the Hospitallers, who serve their own ends and fight with each other as if they were sworn foes. We need substantial financial aid, and it seems that it is time to win over the Byzantine Emperor Manuel to our side. If you would grant your loyal servant's desire by wedding one of the Byzantine princesses, it would be an opportunity for us to form a martial alliance with them and obtain ample money for the costs of our soldiers. They always complain about the delay in their wages, and they cannot be blamed; they need money to provide for themselves and their families. It is unfair to ask them to lay down their lives without providing them with adequate compensation, for money is the lifeblood."

King Baldwin III: "You have convinced me of the importance of my marriage, especially if it will secure the safekeeping of The Kingdom of God, as well as provide a successor from my lineage who will safeguard the kingdom's identity and dominance over its enemies."

Constable Humphrey: "I thank you, Your Grace, for consenting to your loyal servant's proposal. I am personally prepared to be the mediator for choosing a suitable spouse for Your Grace. This is a splendid opportunity for us to preserve the Kingdom of God in the face of perils looming over us from our enemies."

King Baldwin III: "I charge you henceforth to seek out the virtuous woman whom I will take as my bride from among the daughters of our Byzantine kin, our brothers in faith, albeit our difference with them in the nature of the third Lord, the Holy Spirit. They claim that he came from God the Father, while we assert that he came from two Gods, the Father and the Son."

And verily, Constable Humphrey set sail with the Archbishop of Nazareth, Bishop Atard, off to Constantinople to select the fitting wife for the King from among the noblewomen of the Byzantine imperial house, who are close to the Emperor, to enforce that alliance with a potent ally whose aid they are in desperate need of.

It befell that Count Flanders arrived then in the Holy Land with large forces as pilgrims, escorted by his wife Sibylla, sister of the French king Louis VII. King Baldwin III saw the Count, accompanied by his forces, as an opportunity to be seized to achieve a glorious triumph for the Crusaders and impair the power of his enemy Nur al-Din. The King beckoned both Reynald de Chatillon, Prince of Antioch, and Count Raymond III of Tripoli, as well as Thoros the Armenian, to coordinate a large military campaign. The allied forces convened in the city of Antioch to devise a plan for achieving a great military victory.

While the leaders were conferring, they received news of Nur al-Din's demise at the Castle of Inab. However, these were false news; it was later confirmed that Nur al-Din was afflicted by a grave illness that might result in his death. Nur al-Din's forces were struck by chaos and fragmentation as a repercussion of his illness. Still, most of his forces remained faithful to their ailing leader, awaiting his recovery so he could resume the battle against their Crusader enemies.

The Crusader allies saw this as a good opportunity and concurred to impose a siege on the Muslim fortress of Shaizar, a strong fortress on the Orontes River, perched on a lofty hill with a fertile plain lying beneath it. They tightened the siege on the fortress, and the defenders faltered in defending their fortress; many of them even fled. Just when the fortress was about to fall readily into the hands of the Crusaders, while Nur al-Din's followers were occupied with his grave illness, a quarrel arose among the Crusaders about Shaizar's fate. King Baldwin III proposed to grant it to Count Flanders in appreciation of his great efforts during the siege. The Crusader leaders consented, except for Reynald de Chatillon, who set terms to grant his consent; the Count had to swear an oath of submission to him, considering that Shaizar lay within his territorial domain. However, Count Flanders refused to swear an oath of allegiance to anyone but King Baldwin III himself, deeming swearing an oath of allegiance to Prince

Reynald of Antioch or any other prince a great affront to him. Therefore, King Baldwin III had to lift the siege of Shaizar to prevent discord among the Crusader leaders. Once more, the Crusaders wasted an opportunity that was served on a silver platter to them, not taking advantage of Muslims being preoccupied with their leader Nur al-Din's illness.

The Crusader forces then made their way to the city of Antioch and resolved to lay siege to the fortress of Harim, situated only twelve miles away from the city of Antioch. There was a history to this fortress, as it was the fortress Nur al-Din had reclaimed after his triumph over the late Prince of Antioch, Raymond de Poitiers, who perished in the battle of Inab eight years ago as we have previously recounted. The Crusaders managed to intensify the siege on this formidable fortress, compelling the defenders to surrender after valiant resistance, and then they bestowed the fortress upon the Prince of Antioch. Although Count Flanders's wish to govern Shaizar under the sovereignty of King Reynald was denied by Reynald shortly before this event, he still partook in the capture of Harim. The King then departed with his forces back to his kingdom, accompanied by Count Flanders.

It came about then that the senile Patriarch of Jerusalem, Bishop Fulcher, who had reached the age of a hundred years old, passed away on the twentieth of November of 1157 AD. This was the patriarch who journeyed to the Pope several years ago to persuade him of the necessity of subjugating the Hospitallers to him, but he did not succeed in his endeavor, and this group remained independent. What draws attention is the intervention of two women who intervened directly in choosing a new patriarch, Sibylla, wife of Count Flanders, and Joveta, aunt of the King, whom Queen Melisende had made the decision for her to devote herself to monastic life when she was the actual ruler of the kingdom. What was strikingly odd is that the same queen who had volunteered her youngest sister for a life of asceticism and piety devoted her minor son, Baldwin III, to a life of debauchery and indulgence in the arms of promiscuous women. Amalric, dean of the Church of the Holy Sepulcher, was chosen as the successor of Patriarch Fulcher.

Meanwhile, King Nur al-Din had recovered from his illness that lasted for more than a month and regained his health and strength to resume his battle against the Crusaders forthwith, not giving the Crusaders a chance to catch up. He besieged a castle in Suwad Tiberias, located on a steep slope near Baniyas. King Baldwin III marched to meet him, and indecisive clashes took place between the two sides. The warring forces then returned to their positions.

Concurrently, Constable Humphrey was reaping the fruits of his efforts and long negotiations to conclude a political marriage deal with the Byzantines. He chose Princess Theodora, the daughter of Emperor Isaac's brother, who was only thirteen years of age, as a wife for King Baldwin III, who was then thirty years old. The details of this agreement show how much financial benefit the King obtained as a result. According to Byzantine traditions then, the woman's guardian pays the dowry to the husband. Prince Isaac paid Baldwin a hundred thousand gold pieces as dowry for his daughter, as well as ten thousand gold pieces for his daughter's trousseau. While the Emperor paid for the wedding expenses, which amounted to ten thousand gold pieces. With this profitable deal, the Crusader King gained a lot of money and a strong ally, while on his part, he gave Theodora Acre as dowry and some fiefs.

Princess Theodora was married to the King in a grand celebration held in Jerusalem and attended by a crowd of dignitaries from the Byzantine imperial family and relatives of the princess, as well as a large crowd of dignitaries and commoners from the kingdom's subjects. At the same wedding ceremony, which took place in October of 1159 AD, the King crowned his Byzantine wife as Queen over the Kingdom of God. This marriage seemed to have a significant effect on the King, as he stopped violating women's honor in his kingdom, something he never seemed to be ashamed of displaying before.

This dialogue transpired between King Baldwin III and his wife, Queen Theodora, two months after they tied the knot.

King Baldwin III: "These days have been splendid since I wedded the most exquisite woman, both in form and spirit. You possess the virtues of noble morals, tenderness, and a marvelous smile that charms both heart and mind. I have been occupied for the past years with leading and safeguarding the Kingdom of God, and God has rewarded me with this magnificent gift, which has bewitched my mind and thoughts. If only I had known what God had in store for me with this stunning Greek beauty, I would have wedded you long ago, Your Majesty the Queen."

Queen Theodora: "Your Majesty the King, I appreciate your admiration of my beauty and morals, which reflects your noble manners. I am delighted to be married to a noble lord from the most illustrious Frankish lineage, who shares with us the true religion based on the Holy Trinity. We also share the enmity with the Muslims who deny the Divinity of Christ the Lord, and they have occupied many of our lands for five centuries in the Levant, Egypt, and most of Anatolia, to name a few. God chose His elect for the divine project called by the late Pope Urban II, and the Crusaders liberated parts of these lands, such as the Syrian Coast, holy Antioch, and glorious Jerusalem—the Tomb of the Lord who gave His soul as a ransom for our sinful souls."

King Baldwin III: "I aspire for stronger bonds of brotherhood between our peoples and more efficient cooperation to liberate all our lands that the Muslims have stolen. I hope that the actions of some fools, such as Reynald de Chatillon, Prince of Antioch, who violated the safe haven of Cyprus and desecrated its sanctities, allowing his criminal soldiers to rape the nuns in their safe monasteries, do not tarnish our reputation. I deeply regret agreeing to marry Princess Constance to him. I rushed into that marriage because we were in difficult circumstances, particularly when we had the important city of Ascalon under siege, which was weighing heavily on my mind."

Queen Theodora: "Yes, we were all enraged by Reynald's criminal acts, especially His Majesty the Emperor, may God protect him, who will not forgive this fool unless he offers a sincere apology to His Majesty. In fact, His Majesty hoped that you would give this defiant idiot the punishment he very much earned."

King Baldwin III: "It is truly disappointing to witness the rebellion of our followers against our sovereignty. Antioch has seemed to embrace disobedience from the very beginning, ever since it fell into the hands of ungrateful leaders twenty-nine years ago. The troubles began when its prince, Bohemond II, was killed, and events began to unravel. His wife, my late aunt Alice, took charge of its affairs and sent an offer to our Muslim enemy, Atabeg Zengi, proposing submission to his sovereignty. My grandfather, King Baldwin II, was determined and thwarted that great conspiracy that nearly tore apart the Kingdom of God. Unfortunately, my grandfather passed away heartbroken due to his daughter's ingratitude. When my father, King Fulk, ascended to the throne, my aunt Alice defied him too and formed an alliance that involved the Count of Tripoli, Pons son of Bertrand, and Joscelin de Courtenay, Count of Edessa. But my father dismantled that wicked alliance and reestablished his true authority over all parts of the Kingdom of God. However, when my father passed away sixteen years ago, my mother took the reins of power with the assistance of her ill-famed advisor, Constable Manasses. The kingdom's prestige dwindled, as did its sovereignty over the other Crusader states. We gradually lost control of the County of Edessa, and nothing remained of it but remnants, which we ultimately lost seven years ago. Here we are today, in the year 1159 AD, and both Reynald, the guardian of Prince Bohemond III of Antioch, and Raymond III, the Count of Tripoli, have refused to acknowledge my authority since I assumed sole rulership of the kingdom eight years ago. It is as if they fail to grasp the lessons of history, which have repeated themselves time and again."

Queen Theodora: "It is evident that your conflicts run deep. I never imagined that discord could infiltrate this divine realm. Even your mother, Her Majesty the Queen, chose not to attend our wedding ceremony and refuses to meet me, as though I were not her son's wife. I left my family and homeland with high hopes of finding solace in a kind mother-in-law within the Kingdom of God, but it appears that will not be the case."

King Baldwin III: "You may not be aware of the complexities of my relationship with my mother. She assumed the throne after my father passed away when I was a mere boy of thirteen, which is your age now, Your Grace. She cleverly filled my days with trivial matters that kept me from my rightful throne, even after I came of age. When I asserted my rightful claim to rule the kingdom, she denied me that and argued that she was crowned as a partner in power alongside my grandfather, my father, and me when I was a toddler of two. Consequently, we divided the Kingdom of God among us, mother and son. However, as she became increasingly frail due to the misguided counsel of the ill-reputed Manasses, I resolved to wrest authority from her and reunify the kingdom. Her heart still harbors deep bitterness towards me. To make matters worse, when I was blessed to wed you, and I found a Queen for God's domain, envy consumed her. She had been the sole Queen of the land for many years. Your anointment stirred dormant passions and sentiments within her. She was afflicted as if senility had suddenly overcome her."

Queen Theodora: "Now I understand why my mother-in-law, Her Majesty the Queen, avoided our wedding ceremony and why she rebuffs me when I request to visit her. Her heart is grievously wounded, and it has yet to heal, even though two months have passed since our splendid wedding feast. It was only marred by Her Majesty's absence. I will do everything in my power to gain her favor and alleviate the burdens that trouble her, especially her perception that I have come to rival her in ruling the Kingdom of God. For God knows that I arrived here as a humble servant, obedient to God and His loyal pilgrims."

In the year 1160 AD, Byzantine Emperor Manuel issued a decree to reclaim the region of Cilicia under imperial rule. At that time, Cilicia was under the control of Prince Thoros of Armenia, who had defied the might of the Byzantine Empire. This Thoros was also an ally of the Crusader Prince Reynald de Chatillon of Antioch, who had previously insulted the imperial majesty through his assault on the Island of Cyprus, as previously recounted.

The Emperor marched with a vast army to Cilicia, prompting Reynald to hastily approach him, begging for the Emperor's mercy. Reynald offered a degrading apology in line with his vile actions, which the Emperor reluctantly accepted. As a consequence, the Crusader state of Antioch, which had enjoyed independence since its founding sixty-two years earlier, was subjected to Byzantine imperial rule for the first time.

King Baldwin III had foreseen the Emperor's intent to subdue Antioch and sought to mitigate the severity of this subjugation on his people, especially considering their prior resistance to Byzantine authority during Emperor John's rule. Baldwin III paid a visit to the Emperor in Cilicia with his troops in an effort to win his favor.

The Emperor warmly welcomed Baldwin III, treating him as a loyal son, while Reynald was relegated to a lower status. The Emperor then entered Antioch, accompanied by both Reynald and the Crusader King. The people of Antioch did not voice any dissent, as Reynald had prepared them for this bitter fate by humbling himself before the Emperor in Cilicia, even going so far as to bow with utmost humility and beg for pardon. During their visit, King Baldwin III admonished Reynald for his actions against the Emperor and his people in Cyprus. Reynald vowed not to repeat his mistakes. It is possible that the King and the Emperor had agreed to portray the surrender of Crusader Antioch to the Byzantines as a strategic alliance aimed at countering the power of Muslim King Nur al-Din.

The combined armies then advanced toward the city of Aleppo, where Nur al-Din was prepared to face the campaign. Surprisingly, the Emperor did not besiege the city; instead, he engaged in a prisoner exchange with Nur al-Din's forces, after which the allied armies retreated to their respective lands. This demonstrated the Emperor's desire to use his alliance with the Crusaders to benefit the Byzantine Empire. He had achieved a significant goal for his grandfather, Emperor Alexios Komnenos, and his father, Emperor John, that is the subjugation of the ancient city of Antioch under Byzantine imperialism.

This discourse occurred between King Baldwin III and his spouse, Queen Theodora, after the King's return to Jerusalem from his joint military campaign with her uncle, the Byzantine Emperor.

Queen Theodora: "I must express my gratitude, Your Majesty, for your great efforts in mediating between His Majesty the Emperor and his rebellious followers, especially Reynald the fool. I also appreciate your collaboration with the

Emperor in securing the release of our Christian brethren who were held captive by the enemy of Christianity, Nur al-Din."

King Baldwin III: "Your compliments are greatly appreciated, especially for our joint efforts with His Majesty the Emperor to curb Reynald's recklessness, which had tarnished the strong bonds that unite us with our fellow believers in faith and purpose."

Queen Theodora: "I cannot fathom why Princess Constance of Antioch chose that dimwit to be her husband. By marrying him, she made him the ruler of Antioch and the guardian of her young son, Bohemond III, instead of her valiant and noble late husband, Raymond de Poitiers, who bravely defended the Kingdom of God until his death."

King Baldwin III: "I did everything in my power to convince her to marry one of the best, most courageous, and virtuous leaders available. I even summoned her to Tripoli, where I proposed to her in a meeting that included her family, offering her the choice of marrying one of three outstanding leaders. However, she rejected them all and chose Reynald the dimwit."

A few months after this conversation, Reynald launched a raid and pillaged a Christian region located between Marash and Duluk for cattle. These local Christians, though subject to Muslims, lived in harmony. They did not anticipate aggression from the Crusaders of Antioch against their Christian brethren. Reynald seemed to view it as easy loot without considering that God's retribution was imminent. On the twenty-third of November in 1160 AD, he was startled by a Muslim force led by Aleppo's governor, Majd al-Din son of al-Dayeh, who acted as Nur al-Din's deputy. Reynald and his companions were captured, and he paid the price for his recklessness in assaulting Christians in the East, whether they were Byzantines or Armenians.

After their prince was seized, the people of Antioch feared that their city would fall into the hands of King Nur al-Din. Consequently, they sent a plea for assistance to King Baldwin III. What was peculiar is that they did not seek aid from their new lord, Byzantine Emperor Manuel, which suggests that they did not fully acknowledge their submission to the Byzantines. This compelled the King to hesitate and delay sending help, as he sought the Emperor's consent to provide assistance to Antioch.

As the King was preparing to leave his house to rescue Antioch, this dialogue takes place between him and his wife, Queen Theodora.

King Baldwin III: "Reynald has fallen into his evil deeds, and he is now attacking our Armenian brothers who live under the protection of the Muslims. I wish he had been captured sooner, before he spoiled our relations with His Majesty Emperor Manuel. I am bitterly angry with Princess Constance for choosing this fool as her husband; she has burdened us greatly with the responsibility of protecting the state of Antioch from external threats."

Queen Theodora: "Indeed, Reynald deserves imprisonment and humiliation as a just reward for his insult to the nuns on the island of Cyprus when his soldiers violated their honor a few years ago. Princess Constance bears some responsibility for choosing that moron. But what is important now is that the people of Antioch need someone to save them before they fall into the hands of Nur al-Din, just as the people of Edessa fell sixteen years ago into the hands of his father, Zengi."

King Baldwin III: "I will do my best to protect the state of Antioch, for its fall into the hands of the Muslims also means the end of the Kingdom of God and the entire Crusader entity. However, it pains me that I have to march my forces to aid Antioch and be deprived of your company and the sight of this beautiful face that has captured my heart and thoughts. But rest assured that my absence will not last long, except in cases of utmost necessity."

Queen Theodora: "I pray to God to protect you and bring you back safely to me and to safeguard the Kingdom of God from the plots of our enemies."

King Baldwin III then marched with his forces, entered the city of Antioch, and entrusted its affairs to the patriarch of its church and Princess Constance as a guardian for her minor son, Bohemond, the son of Raymond de Poitiers. He returned to Jerusalem shortly after ensuring its defenses, where Queen Theodora was eagerly waiting for him.

In 1160 AD, an opportunity arose when the Empress of the Byzantine Emperor Manuel passed away. Seeking to strengthen his alliance with the Emperor, King Baldwin III decided to send a messenger to consult with him about a potential marriage to one of the Crusader princesses. The messenger was instructed to propose Princess Melisende, the daughter of King Baldwin III's aunt Hodierna and sister of Count Raymond III of Tripoli.

However, the Emperor's messenger stayed in Tripoli for an entire year, leaving King Baldwin III eagerly awaiting a final answer regarding his endorsement for Princess Melisende. It was rumored that the Emperor had a change of heart due to questions raised about the moral character of Melisende's mother, Hodierna. Interestingly, Count Raymond III had spent a significant amount of money preparing his sister for marriage to the Emperor, who had yet to make a definitive decision on the matter. Even more amusing, the Emperor ultimately chose to marry Princess Maria, the daughter of Princess Constance from her previous marriage to Raymond de Poitiers. Maria was favored for her beauty over Melisende. This political marriage stirred mixed emotions, angering Raymond III but pleasing Constance and her daughter Maria.

King Baldwin III achieved his goal of strengthening his alliance with the Byzantine Emperor through this marriage, although he wouldn't see the immediate benefits of this alliance.

A grand ceremony was held in Antioch to celebrate Emperor Manuel's marriage to Maria, attended by dignitaries and commoners of the kingdom, with King Baldwin III acting as an agent for the bride as well as the Emperor.

On the eleventh of September 1161 AD, King Baldwin III was on his way to the Iron Bridge fortress, located six miles away from Antioch, to oversee its repair. However, during his journey, he received the news of his mother's death. Strikingly, this event filled him with a profound grief that he had never experienced before. As he reflected on his beautiful yet bittersweet memories with her, he couldn't help but blame himself for the harsh actions he had taken when he stripped her of all the powers that her father, King Baldwin II, had granted her.

With the passing of Queen Melisende, an important chapter in the history of the Crusader entity in the East came to a close. She had ruled for twenty years in the Kingdom of God, and although she received unprecedented praise from prominent Crusader chronicler William of Tyre for her significant role in the history of the Crusader entity in the East, the experience of women's rule had its negative and serious consequences. Perhaps the most significant of these consequences was the weakening of political and military unity within this entity. This period saw the county of Edessa removed from the political map, and the Kingdom of Jerusalem was on the brink of disintegration due to the political division that had been agreed upon by King Baldwin III and Queen Melisende in 1151 AD. While the King later took measures to rectify the situation and reunite the kingdom through force and cunning, as we explained before, it was too late to fully correct his mother's mistakes.

Two weeks after his mother's death, this conversation takes place between King Baldwin III and Queen Theodora in Antioch.

Queen Theodora: "Although I never had the chance to meet Her Majesty Queen Melisende in person, her loss deeply saddens me, almost as if I had lost my own mother at that moment. I had wished to see her and forge a friendship, especially after she fell victim to that illness that weakened her memory and affected her body and mind. However, despite my persistence, Her Majesty refused to see me. This rejection hurt me deeply, but I find solace in being married to Your Majesty."

King Baldwin III: "Her loss has deeply affected me. I regret not showing her enough gratitude. She was the eldest and most favored child of my grandfather King Baldwin II, and the rightful heir to the kingdom. She was crowned queen shortly before my grandfather's passing. During my father King Fulk's reign, she became the ruler of the kingdom. After my father's death, she continued to rule alone and even maintained her guardianship over me, even after I came of age. However, I made the decision to defy her and take over the kingdom as its sole leader. I was so cruel that I even bombarded her castle in Jerusalem with catapults. How I regret my harshness towards her. I pray to God for her mercy and forgiveness."

Five months after Queen Melisende's passing, her son King Baldwin III also departed, in January of 1162 AD, due to an excessive dose of laxative medicine. When he took that remedy, he sensed that his end was near, so he traveled from Antioch to his capital. However, he breathed his last in Beirut before reaching his capital. Thus, the reign of this King, who took over the kingdom during its most challenging period, came to an end. It was a time when several women had ruled it, with the most prominent being his mother, Melisende, who departed this world before her son.

While the Crusader entity was grappling with internal disintegration and military weakness at that time, the Islamic East was united in the Levant under the leadership of King Nur al-Din Mahmoud. The new Crusader King, Amalric, would stand against Nur al-Din's ambitions. However, the balance of power would eventually shift in favor of the Muslims under Nur al-Din and later King Saladin al-Ayyubi. The era of women's rule in the Crusader kingdom served as an opportunity for the Muslims to unite their forces and launch a sweeping attack against the Crusader entity, aiming to uproot it from the East. This would indeed happen twenty-two years after King Baldwin III's death in the famous Battle of Hattin. It seems that the experience of Western European women assuming power in the Islamic East was an unprecedented phenomenon in the Middle Ages, as Western women had rarely ruled in Latin Europe at that time.